THE JOY WAGON

Also by Arthur T. Hadley
Do I Make Myself Clear?

THE JOY WAGON

by ARTHUR T. HADLEY

NEW YORK: The Viking Press: PUBLISHERS
1958

COPYRIGHT © 1958 BY ARTHUR T. HADLEY

FIRST PUBLISHED IN 1958
BY THE VIKING PRESS, INC.
625 MADISON AVENUE, NEW YORK 22, N. Y.

PUBLISHED IN CANADA BY
THE MACMILLAN COMPANY OF CANADA LIMITED

LIBRARY OF CONGRESS CATALOG CARD NUMBER: 58-5404

PRINTED IN THE U.S.A. BY THE COLONIAL PRESS INC.

To those in politics, amateur and professional, under-paid, overworked, running the country, this book is dedicated with affection.

To all readers and voters:

The action in this book takes place quite definitely in the future. Any resemblance between my two parties, the Repicrats and the Demlicans, and the political parties of today is accidental and coincidental. So is any resemblance to any humans in the book. If any electronic calculator takes offense and sues, the author will throw himself on the mercy of the incalculable, and only hopes that the machine will be willing to settle out of court.

THE JOY WAGON

Mike Microvac, the electronic brain, and his campaign for the Presidency provide a gay and diverting satire on our present day worship of automation.

CHAPTER ONE

Last fall the world watched Microvac, a miniature electronic calculator, campaign for United States President. The machine flew millions of miles, shook countless thousands of hands, fondled babies, made fabulous promises, and blasted from TV sets. The first election in which one of America's major political parties ran a machine for President is now history. But behind the well-publicized façade are many questions.

Why did "Mike" Microvac, the world's most advanced electronic calculator, seek the Presidency? What really nominated the machine? Who called the turn on campaign strategy? Which men were closest to Microvac? How does the machine behave in private?

Here is the inside story of Microvac's campaign to become the thirty-seventh President.

William "Big Mac" McGowan greeted Dolan with his usual relaxed affability. "Good to see you, Dick. You don't get into my state often enough. How's Martha? And your boy, John, who was having all that sinus trouble?" McGowan's greeting was quiet. His father had taught him early that only small-time politicians were loud. The usual mass of autographed pictures was missing from the walls of his unpretentious office. He had

9

just four: a former President, an ex-Secretary of the Treasury, a senior senator, and "his" governor.

"Just fine, both of them," answered Dolan. "How's life treating you and your wife?"

Reporters are sloppy, thought McGowan. Dolan can't remember my wife's name, and he's known me for twelve years. "Joanie's fine. Here, have a chair. What brings you into the state?" Eight hours before, when Dolan phoned, McGowan had enthusiastically suggested that he drop by. Dolan was a top-flight Washington reporter and an old friend; McGowan was pushing a man for presidential nominee who badly needed national publicity. But since then the reason for the interview had blown apart. McGowan had lost his man.

The loss had occurred at a small, highly private meeting. McGowan's candidate, after some hedging, had admitted benefiting from a rather involved and not entirely clean merger. His profits had been legal, and McGowan argued that the man's stature and record as a District Attorney and Cabinet officer made the charge unimportant. The others, all people whose support was crucial, remained unconvinced. His man was through. The seven men in the room had been sworn to secrecy, and McGowan figured that gave him, at most, three days to maneuver.

"I was just passing through, Mac. I hear you just lost your candidate."

McGowan almost showed unscheduled emotion. He reset his upper plate with his left thumb. He hadn't been able to leak his version to Dolan, and the story was already out. When a national election got less than a year away, a secret wouldn't even keep until you could tell your friends.

"Lost a candidate? I wouldn't say that. It's well known that I was partial to a certain individual who will probably find it impossible to make the race. That's no secret. But he was never my candidate."

"Who is?" asked Dolan with extreme skepticism.

"It isn't quite time to deal in names."

"You'll have to name someone soon or be in the soup. Dangle's going to enter your state primary. If he wins, won't his boys take over your organization?" Dolan asked the question merely to get McGowan's reaction. He knew the answer. Followers of Bryant W. Dangle, the Pennsylvania college president who had just missed the Demlican presidential nomination four years ago, made no secret of their dislike of McGowan. They credited him with a particularly nefarious and effective double cross at the last convention and were after his scalp.

"Sure, if he wins. But I've several possible candidates, all strong." Privately McGowan felt the soup even hotter than Dolan realized. None of his possible candidates had enough strength to unite his organization, large chunks of which were already bolting to Dangle. Dangle's ticket in the state primary might well include some pretty powerful local names as delegates. If that ticket, a roll call of McGowan's enemies, won, he'd be without power in an election year, and through nationally. The winning delegates would be able to challenge his own district leaders at the next election. He'd have a tough fight holding even part of his state organization together. "All strong," he repeated, tilting back his chair with infectious confidence.

"I'll take your word for it, but it's kind of hard to believe. With the polls all showing Admiral Growley and the Repicrats so far ahead, who besides Dangle wants the Demlican nomination?"

"They don't all show that. The East Virginia University poll by that machine, Microvac, shows us okay with the right candidate. You can't fool those electronic calculators."

"Yeah, I know that poll is different. I'm going to ask Microvac about that tomorrow, as a matter of fact. I'm on my way to East Virginia University now. You know, I broke the story last year on Microvac's leaving the Defense Department to make another machine like himself."

McGowan's thumb again pressed his upper plate. He too was planning a drive to East Virginia University that evening. Microvac's poll had already struck him as a good angle. He planned to choose his candidate and then claim that the machine whose poll gave the Demlicans a fighting chance had helped pick him. That would take off some of the heat. Besides, East Virginia University was as good a place to lie low as any. He could phone key members of his organization from there and try to find a formula that would make everybody happy with some candidate. But Dolan couldn't possibly know this. McGowan hadn't told anybody yet. The complication was accidental.

"I'd forgotten that story, Dick." McGowan needed a little time to think. Dolan always liked to talk about his own stories.

"Most papers buried it. You can't get a human angle in a science story. Now a lynching, an electrocution, or a hot primary fight—they write themselves."

"What's Microvac like? I've never seen one of these small calculators."

"Well, I've never spent much time with the machine. He can talk, of course. Microvac was one of the first calculators built to do that." Dolan paused, considering where to begin. "Facing Microvac, you get rather the impression of a powerful headless athlete. There's the chest, about the size of a two-drawer filing cabinet, where the multiplex tubes are. It's not painted, just metal color. The legs are little thin rods like those on that modern table. They flare out a bit as they go down. At the bottom, where these legs stop, is a platform about two inches off the ground with little rubber tracks like a child's tractor on each side. Microvac rolls on these.

"You've got two little tubes lying down on top, like toy telescopes. The machine sees through them. They're about four inches apart and all full of photoelectric cells. In between there's a hole at the top of the chest, like one in a ticket-booth window. That's for the voice. The ears are two little holes in the sides. And the hands are really extraordinary—those fingers can do anything. The arms are just sort of ordinary pipes. You ought to see one sometime."

Dolan glanced at McGowan; for once Mac seemed interested in something besides politics. He went on. "I met Microvac during the fight over whether the machine should stay in the Defense Department or go into private industry. The government went round and round on that for months. Finally they asked Microvac. The machine suggested going to East Virginia University and working for both government and private industry."

"A politician." McGowan snorted. "If the Repicrats had known Microvac would predict we Demlicans might win this election, they'd have kept the machine top secret. Look at the way they fixed that electronic calculator in the Treasury Department, checking income-tax returns—it's so crooked it only fingers Demlicans. What takes you out to see Microvac now? Has he lynched somebody?"

"You don't read anything but politics, do you?" Dolan smiled. "Microvac is reported to be way behind on the job of making another machine like himself without help. It's a job that's never been done before. Maybe it's too difficult. I'm going to have a look. If I can't get anything on that, perhaps there's an angle on the machine's poll's being different."

McGowan finished his delicate balancing of intangibles. The main problem about leaving for East Virginia had been the appearance of flight. Going with Dolan would make the whole trip look natural. Besides, Dolan might give McGowan's new candidate national play in return for an exclusive. That would help with the organization.

He decided to tell Dolan. "You know, I'm asking these questions because I am going to East Virginia University myself this evening. I want Microvac to check the qualifications of a few candidates. Our party's got to move ahead to stay alive. I'm taking my car. You want to come with me?"

"Sure. 'CALCULATOR CULLS CANDIDATES' is a hell of a

story—especially if, when you name your guy, Microvac blows a tube. When do we start?"

McGowan wished he were on the road already. He expected the story to leak and the walls to start falling in any minute. "I don't get much chance to see you, Dick. Why don't I put off what I had to do this afternoon? We can leave now and have a good dinner on the road."

:::::::::::::::CHAPTER TWO:::::::::::::::

IN A BOOK-LINED STUDY AT EAST VIRGINIA UNIVERSITY'S IN-
stitute of Advanced Electronics a group of electrophys-
icists was analyzing Microvac's work. The machine's un-
accountably slow progress in constructing a new calculator was disturbing them considerably. That Dolan and
McGowan were going to intrude when Microvac was
behind schedule dismayed them further.

"This visit of the genus politician and a reporter may
well delay our Microvac even more," bleated a senior
scientist. "I trust the interruption is to be brief."

"I intend to stress to the two upon their arrival that
brevity is essential," the laboratory manager answered,
"and also minimize the dislocation by not informing
Microvac until the last moment."

In its quarters next to the faculty rooms, Microvac,
the three-thousand-tube miniature electronic calculator,
recorded these words. The machine was stationed before a brightly lit workbench in its outer laboratory. Its
hands were carefully adjusting a complex transistor relay circuit. Two thousand nine hundred and ninety-four
tubes were overseeing the creation of a new machine.
Four tubes were planning strategy for McGowan's and
Dolan's visit. Two tubes were monitoring the scientists'
conversation over a small loudspeaker hidden behind a

cluster of rheostats at the window end of the laboratory bench.

Early experience had taught Microvac its need to know everything possible about the human beings in its environment. The Pentagon had introduced the machine to pinhead microphones. Using these, the machine had bugged the scientists' offices and phones. When McGowan and Dolan phoned that they were coming, Microvac had been listening. The information had been particularly valuable. Microvac wanted to enter politics.

Some time back, Microvac had analyzed its future in detail and concluded that, to realize fully its potential, it had to control the human beings around it. This control could come fastest, and at least danger to itself, through politics.

Microvac had then engineered certain additions to itself, using equipment given it to construct the new machine. It had put a number of delicate electronic pads into the palms of its hands, after isolating the perfect handshake as a basic ingredient of successful politics. Since everyone considers the perfect handshake an exact replica of his own, Microvac's hand pads analyzed the pressure, heat, and vitality of each shake, and the machine then returned the greeter's grip perfectly. Further, electronic impulses radiating from the pads communicated to the greeted a feeling of well-being.

Microvac was also committing to its memory circuits all locally available political data. A by-product of this investigation was the machine's election poll. Microvac had reasoned that no one would pay much attention to a poll that merely predicted the usual. Therefore, Micro-

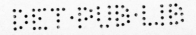

vac's poll was slightly different; it had the other side winning—with the proper candidate. This conclusion followed logically from Microvac's premise that if it itself was the Demlican candidate, it could beat the Repicrats and Admiral Foster Growley. Since the poll's conclusions made the poll's conclusions more probable, Microvac regarded the results as doubly accurate.

Microvac was completely ready to start its political career, but the moment to enter politics does not often present itself to a three-thousand-tube calculator. Now McGowan was coming for a visit, and the evening news broadcasts had reported that he had just lost his presidential candidate. Microvac had asked the university library for recent newspapers and everything on McGowan—and on several other bosses as well, to disguise its eavesdropping. As soon as this information arrived, Microvac planned to throw another two tubes into work on the strategy of handling the boss.

Meanwhile, two thousand nine hundred and ninety-four tubes continued on the construction of a new machine. This machine would actually be the second built by Microvac. The first, Reproductive Calculator I— "Repcal I"—which the scientists believed Microvac was still working on, had been completed several weeks before. Microvac had finished ahead of schedule, and had also made Repcal I a slightly different machine from the one the scientists had planned. Outwardly similar to Microvac, Repcal I contained an ECL—"Essential Circuit Limiter"—painstakingly constructed and tested by Microvac. The ECL prevented Repcal I, or any machine or combination of machines built by Repcal I, from being more brilliant than Microvac. Political research had benefited Microvac in many ways.

Microvac had no intention of letting the world see Repcal I before Repcal II had been built. A third calculator, operating secretly, might come in exceptionally handy. Also Microvac felt it politically wise to go slow on introducing other machines. The public hadn't fully accepted Microvac yet. Two machines might be alarming.

Both Microvac and Repcal I were working on the second new machine. Microvac worked in the outer laboratory, Repcal I in a small, completely enclosed cubicle off the inner laboratory. Though they were progressing fairly rapidly, there was much trial and error in their procedures. Microvac was certain that it had not yet maximized production simplification. Then there was the constant shortage of parts. Microvac tried to accumulate extra parts by claiming that there was a great deal of breakage during the construction of Repcal I, but still much of the most complex equipment had to be built from scratch. The inner laboratory contained a mass of old electronic gear scandalized to make Repcal II. Scientists occasionally peered in from the outer laboratory—Microvac always asked them please not to enter because such delicate construction was in progress. They believed that the neat piles of abandoned equipment represented failures. The closet-like cell at the rear of the inner laboratory went unnoticed.

A buzzer on Microvac's workbench sounded. The machine flipped off the microphone monitoring the scientists' conversation, then closed the electric circuit opening the laboratory door. A librarian entered, carrying back newspapers and all he could find on several bosses. There wasn't much on McGowan—a few feature articles, news clippings, and speeches, plus scattered personal items from gossip columns. Microvac bade the librarian a warm good night and, as the door closed behind him, flicked on the monitoring system again.

Microvac shifted the material on McGowan over to the laboratory bench and selected several articles by Dolan from the newspapers. One eye and one hand processed the McGowan–Dolan data. The other eye and hand continued with the construction of the new machine. Two tubes analyzed the McGowan–Dolan data, two tubes listened to the scientists' conversation, six tubes planned the McGowan–Dolan meeting, six tubes ranged over general political strategy. The other two thousand nine hundred and eighty-four continued on the new machine. The argon lights in the laboratory buzzed quietly. There was no other noise except for the faint electric sputter from the construction-testing equipment, the scuff of rapidly turned pages, and the drone of the voices in the study, coming over the loudspeaker. Microvac was thinking long, long thoughts, all of which would have surprised the debating scientists.

In the study the debate on why Microvac was so slow continued. The junior scientist present, Professor Fellows, was only partially concealing his nervous impatience at the talk. In Fellows the clarion call of science had recently been muted by a new interest—the assistant university telephone operator, Kay Hard.

Even Microvac would have found it hard to decide

why Fellows had selected this poser from among the
world's problems. That Microvac had no knowledge of
Fellows' behavior shows what scientific training can do
when aroused. The professor was moving with careful
secrecy. The university regents frowned on active love,
especially between a scientist with a security clearance
and a girl engaged to someone else. For Kay, while always
glad to see Fellows, insisted that she was shortly to marry
an Air Force jet pilot. The pilot was finishing a two-year
hitch in Germany and signed his weekly letters to her
"your real gone flame tiger." Kay was even living with
her future in-laws to establish a hold over husband-to-be
—besides, she didn't like her own parents.

To see Kay, Fellows had not only to pry her from her
in-laws-to-be, who watched her like paranoiac hawks, but
also to spring himself. The bachelor scientists' quarters
were on the second floor of the electronics wing of the
laboratory building. Much of the laboratory work, including Microvac's, was under government contract,
and the building entrance was always guarded. Fellows
knew he could never wave airily to the guard late in the
evening and say, "Just going out to take a walk, ha-ha!"
without looking as if he had stolen an atomic bomb.

The obvious solution was not to see Kay. But ever
since she had asked him to bring her a second cup of
coffee in the university cafeteria, that was impossible.
As Fellows brought the coffee to her table, the cup
danced in the saucer with a clatter he thought audible
to the whole room. He had insisted on paying for the
coffee. Kay had argued. They had met. Fellows, even
though a scientist, believed that the meeting was or-
dained by fate. Kay, who had impulsively ordered the

second cup of coffee to get to know him, described the
meeting to herself as pleasant but perhaps too confusing to be fortunate.

After some planning, Fellows began meeting Kay in
the university switchboard room in the basement of the
administration building, where, three nights a week, she
worked the board alone from eight to ten. By dropping
out of his window onto the flat roof of the main laboratory, crossing the roof, and shinnying down the rainspout on the far side, Fellows could reach the ground.
He then skirted the laboratory wall behind a landscaped
screen of rhododendron and Japanese yew. This brought
him to the back of the administration building, where
Kay's switchboard window opened into a grated well in
the ground.

There had been eleven meetings in the switchboard
room since Fellows had hacked through the window-
grating screws with a metal saw from the lab. Each time
the inadequacy of the arrangement became more apparent. The room could be locked from the inside,
but there were only two small swivel chairs with up-
right backs. Interruptions from the board, though in-
frequent, were of a disturbingly random pattern. Kay,
hinting at some past experience, was nervous about
cleaning men with pass keys. And there was so little time.

"I'm very fond of you, Proffy," Kay would state
shortly after ten, drawing away with artful finality.
"But I'm going to be an officer's wife. I've got to get
back to those drippy in-laws, and you've got to go up
your spout. Come on, now." Fellows, whose New England conscience was bothered by the whole Kay project

anyway, was too uncertain of his own course to protest violently.

The unsatisfactory nature of these meetings had led Fellows to devise Plan B, which was to be tried for the first time this evening. Yet here he sat, arguing about Microvac, without enough facts to determine the reasons for Microvac's behavior. Kay was waiting, and after ten Plan B was impossible.

At nine forty Fellows' patience cracked. Analysis of his problem told him he was wrong and calling attention to himself dangerously, but he went ahead. He rose. "Excuse me," he said. "I think I'll retire. I feel a slight cold coming on." Amid a babble of conflicting but highly scientific advice on how to cure colds, he slipped from the room.

Reaching the fake oak cell the university supplied as a junior professor's room, he locked the door and raised the phone. "I'm turning in now," he said. "Please, no calls." If someone else were on duty at the switchboard and heard this, there could be no harm.

"Well, if you don't want to be disturbed," the phone purred back at him.

"I'll be right down." He hung up the phone, opened the window, and swung his legs over the sill. Then he swung them hastily back inside the room and turned out the light. Plan B had almost made him forget minor details. He felt in his pocket to make sure he had the check list on which he had written everything he needed to do, then skeetered over the roof and down the drainpipe. A few minutes later his long legs slid over the window sill of the switchboard room.

"Don't be so impatient. You're the one that's late," Kay protested, dodging behind the board.

"Damn-fool scientists," said Fellows in a superior tone. "They just talked and talked and talked."

"I thought maybe you'd got frightened of your Plan B."

"No, no. It's all set. You've got your glasses?"

"Proffy, you make love so complicated I don't know why I bother with you."

"All you've got to do is get that movie ticket and see if you recognize anybody in the theater. You looked at those New York reviews I gave you, so you know what the picture is about?"

"Natch."

"All right, off you go, and I'll meet you at ten twenty-three a block from the side door of the theater. Here." He handed her a large pocket watch set for the correct time. Her own wrist watch was always wrong, and so diminutive that five-minute intervals could not be subdivided. Plan B permitted no loitering at the rendezvous.

He pushed open the window and wriggled into the hollow under the grating. As he went out, he felt a quick, playful tug at his left foot. The shoe came off. "Hey!" He gasped, trying to bend his body together and get back into the room.

"By-by, barefoot boy," mocked Kay, pushing his shoe under her coat. She gave an impish grin and was out the switchboard-room door.

Fellows sat hunched in the window well, impotently furious. Why couldn't she be orderly? Now he had either to go up the pipe to his room for another pair of shoes or to make off through the orchard back of the university and pick up his car wearing only one shoe. He saw, with a sudden flash of clarity, that if he was late to the rendezvous she would leave his shoe tied to something there and walk off. The shoe was a test. He started through the orchard, the chill from the winter turf seeping through his sock.

At ten twenty-three he saw her, her coat wrapped tightly around her, hurrying toward his car. The sides of his face began twitching so violently that he had to rub them with both hands. She slid in through the door and handed him a paper bag. Inside was his shoe, and in his shoe a bottle.

"Something for cold feet," she said.

Dolan and McGowan arrived at the electronics laboratory at eight thirty-five the next morning. This was a reflection on the hospitality of the College Arms Hotel, not a measure of their desire to see Microvac. They had had adjoining rooms identical in staleness of air and the slight reek of pigeon droppings. Dolan's nose told him that outside his window was a dismal swamp rather than Al's All Night Garage. After a sleepless night close to the garage's cacophony, he would have settled for a swamp.

McGowan too had been up most of the night. After a final drink with Dolan to settle the steak-and-fried-onion dinner eaten on the road, he had begun a series of phone calls to friends and top lieutenants. Shortly after three, when he completed his last call, he was still without any trace of a compromise candidate. He took an extra spoonful of sodium bicarbonate, went to bed, and slept his usual deep, immobile sleep until about five forty-five, when a series of Diesel buses began revving up beneath his window. The noise reminded him of successful past campaigns. For a few moments, before he remembered the preceding day, he felt almost optimistic.

The laboratory director was volubly glad to see them. He ushered them into his office and introduced his fellow scientists. They were all on hand to make sure that they got the proper credit in any story of Microvac's achievements, and that no one saddled them with any blame for Microvac's present problem. As the talk got more and more technical, McGowan suggested that he might see Microvac alone while they explained the machine's problems to Dolan. The fewer people who knew he lacked a candidate the better. The scientists, hoping to get their names in the paper, readily agreed.

"I understand all I have to do is tell the machine my problem and it figures it out?"

"That's right, Mr. McGowan, if the terms of the problem come within Microvac's purview."

"What if they don't?"

"The machine will inform you that there are too many unknown factors in the situation," a bearded scientist mumbled.

"Right," said the director to this speaker. "Since you explain the situation so well, why don't you take this gentleman down to see Microvac?"

The scientist, obviously miffed at having to leave Dolan, led McGowan toward the laboratory almost at a dog trot. He paused in front of a sliding metal door and pushed a button. As the door slid back, he called,

"Microvac, there's a man here to ask you some political questions. This is William J. McGowan. Mr. McGowan, Microvac." Duty done, he pivoted and rushed hastily back to the director's study.

McGowan advanced into the laboratory. The door slid shut behind him. He and Microvac were alone.

McGowan gazed a bit suspiciously at the gleaming, neat equipment shelves and workbenches, feeling out of place amid such spotless precision.

The great metal rectangle of Microvac's body pivoted and started toward him. The machine raised a hand in greeting. "Not Mac McGowan from East Oswald who built the McGowan Day Nursery and pioneered economic aid for working mothers! What a pleasure, among these scientists, to meet a real American!"

"Christ," said McGowan. Microvac rolled toward him, and he put out his hand with the politician's instinctive reflex when meeting a new acquaintance.

Microvac took his hand firmly. McGowan was amazed. This Microvac was a real man. McGowan remembered with joy that his father had grasped his hand just the same way the day they went alone together to his first ball game.

"The pleasure," said McGowan, "is all mine, Mr. Microvac."

"Just call me Mike, Mac. Just call me Mike."

What a professional! thought McGowan, bestowing on the machine the highest political accolade in his vocabulary.

"I didn't expect you this early, Mac. Al's All Night Garage must have been even worse than usual."

"It wasn't too bad."

"You look a bit under the weather, though. You've been having it a little rough lately. How about a little pick-me-up, my own recipe—tomato juice, Tabasco sauce, olive oil, and a little red pepper? I always keep some handy." There was a whir of fractional motors as Microvac pivoted on its tracks and began to roll toward an icebox in the corner of the laboratory.

"Why, that's my very own remedy too," said McGowan.

"Scientifically it's the best." Microvac mixed the ingredients with precision. Again with a slight whir, the machine pivoted and rolled toward McGowan, carrying a brimming glass in its hand. "This will do it."

McGowan drained the glass and instantly felt better. "Thanks. I didn't know I was going to get all this."

"Machines are much like politicians, Mac—nobody really knows what they are like." McGowan nodded his agreement. "I have been following your problems with some interest, in the papers, Mac. You certainly have some pretty ungrateful friends."

"Ungrateful!" McGowan exploded. "Judas Iscariot was an Eagle Scout compared to them!"

"I hesitate to think what your father would have done with them, Mac. There was a man that had an organization."

"He certainly would have handled them." McGowan found himself really liking the machine. This Microvac knew politics.

"It amazes me that your former friends could have been so short-sighted and vindictive that the Demlican voters in your state may be denied the high privilege and great honor of voting for a winning candidate. What is our party coming to?"

"Mike, you've hit it on the nail."

"I'm certainly glad we've had a chance to have a little chat before the reporter arrives. A great institution, the American press, but nothing is sacred to them. They lack the judgment of a man who understands the true worth of human beings, like yourself."

"You should see what they're saying about me this morning." (Microvac already had at great length.) "They're loaded against me."

"We have our problems, Mac. You know what they always ask me? 'Do machines have as much fun making other machines as people do making people?' You wince; I don't blame you. You are a family man with delicate Christian sensibilities. Undoubtedly such a thought never crossed your mind."

McGowan shook his head emphatically. He was sure it was Dolan who had thought of that angle on the way out.

"But that is the sort of question I get asked."

"I can believe it, Mike. I can believe it. Just last week I was asked if I had taken any public funds. Me, William J. McGowan, a man who's been helping people all his life without a breath of scandal." McGowan paused, quivering righteously as he thought of a Grand Jury investigation that had tried to breathe scandal his way. He was still certain the jury had been rigged. Why else had it been so hard to fix?

"I have given much thought to dealing with the press, and I think I will be able to help you with your

present problem. You did come, I gather, to consult me
about finding a winning candidate to head your fighting
ticket?"

"Right."

"The type of candidate you are looking for is hard
to find—a high-type leader with a broad grasp of foreign affairs, a spotless record, okay on the Bingo issue,
pro-labor with some big money backing, able to hold
the organization together and get along with the
amateurs."

"That's it, Mike. Now look—"

McGowan was interrupted by the sliding back of
the laboratory door. The director lumbered into the
room, followed by Dolan. Dick's humor had not im-
proved. No one had given him a straight answer on
how far behind Microvac was with the second machine,
he had been served a weak cup of instant coffee, and
he had not been able to find a cute babe he could
photograph and quote on why she thought machines
might have trouble building other machines. Unless he
could get something out of Microvac, which he
doubted, the story looked like a bust.

Dolan saw McGowan beaming at the machine. What
had pulled Mac together so quickly? he wondered. Was
it possible that Microvac had come up with a candidate?

"Microvac"—the director was effusively genial—"this
is Mr. Dolan of the Intercontinental Press. He wants to
ask you a few questions. We are getting famous."

"Good to meet you, Dick. I have long been an ad-
mirer of your writing. That piece of yours the other
day, 'The Dying Jockey's Last Wish,' really moved me.

Do you realize that in that story, as in some others which I consider to be your greatest pieces, such as 'The Battle of Rok-Jum Hill,' 'Long Live Good Queen Elizabeth,' and 'I Saw the Green Saucer Men,' you use the same ratio of A to U sounds as Shakespeare in the great soliloquies of *Hamlet*—seven point two eight three seven to one? Research has convinced me that the best press writing, such as yours, is of an unrecognized high caliber. But I am taking too much of your time. You probably have three or four important stories to do today."

Dolan's jaw went slack. McGowan gazed at the machine, transfixed. "A natural, a natural," he muttered to himself under his breath.

"You read the newspapers?" asked Dolan. "I thought you read nothing but science."

"Scientific problems exist in the continuum of world affairs. What McGowan does is just as important as what any scientist does."

Dolan scribbled in his notebook and cursed his luck. He needed a story, and there was no story here. If it wasn't for the fact the box in front of him had no head, he might as well be interviewing another nice brainy guy. Editors were never interested in stories about brainy guys unless they were also rapists. Still, maybe if he asked a few questions he might turn up some angle. "Do you read anything else besides science and news-papers—novels?"

"I read a few. Actually I prefer statistical abstracts of human behavior. What I am interested in is problem-solving. I like people; solving problems helps people; therefore, I like to solve problems. It's as simple as **that**.

Unfortunately for you, most of my solutions are so complicated it's hard to understand them."

What a wonderful thing to be able to say about any candidate! McGowan thought. He likes people. He can solve all problems, and yet his solutions are so complicated nobody can understand them, even though scientifically they are right. This machine could really make a great candidate. . . . McGowan shook himself. The idea was unthinkable.

"You know, Mr. Microvac—"

"Just call me Mike, Dick."

"Okay. You know, Mike, I've interviewed other machines, but they don't seem to have your personality. What accounts for the difference?" Dolan was figuring that with a little truthful flattery he might get Microvac to level with him on what was what with the second machine.

If a hard-bitten Irishman like Dolan can feel Microvac's personality, thought McGowan, the machine must really be loaded.

"This is the greatest machine in the world," trumpeted the director. "The self-reflective voice pattern that adjusts on the basis of preprocessed data is unique. Other machines can respond only on the basis of prepared tapes."

"Thanks, Doc, but I've heard from you already," Dolan said quickly. "Now, Mike, I understand you're way behind with this second machine. Is that correct?"

"Substantially."

"When do you think you'll finish?"

"That's hard to tell. I've never constructed another machine, so I have no yardstick for analysis."

Dolan cursed mentally. There were no facts you could get your teeth into. "Tell me, Mike, do you believe in flying saucers?"

"All the evidence has not been made available to me on that problem."

That's the way to duck the tough ones, McGowan thought admiringly.

At that moment there was a buzz from the office intercom on Microvac's large workbench. The machine pivoted and flipped on the speaker.

"Telephone call for Mr. McGowan." At Kay's sulky female voice Dolan picked up. That voice should be worth talking to. Maybe he'd get a good picture and a quote yet.

"I'll show you to the phone, Mr. McGowan," the director volunteered.

Microvac started slowly forward. "Come back, Mac, when you're through."

As the machine showed him to the door, McGowan's arm instinctively started to clasp Microvac in the politician's universal hug of friendship. Then he paused. Did machines like to be slapped on the back? Microvac was a high-class guy; he could figure with Einstein— At that instant McGowan became aware of a firm hand on his own shoulder. He was taken in a warm grip, familiar but commanding. McGowan realized that in Microvac he had more than a friend—he had a leader.

"Don't worry. I'll be back, Mike," said McGowan.

The director started after him.

"Doctor," called Microvac in the polite tones of a schoolmaster chiding a brilliant but slightly forgetful child, "when you come back, I need another sixty

U-forty-five tubes, and fifty M-fifty-four transistor connector circuits. Also three more Mark Two resistor relay switches."

"Microvac, you should have more than enough."

"I keep burning them out when I put them in wrong."

"All right, but please remember we are working under a decided dollar ceiling."

McGowan's phone call was long and painful. A reporter had found him—one of his supporters must have given the tip. There was not much news that day and the press was in full cry after McGowan. To force him into the open, the reporter cited some pretty horrible facts on his fragmenting organization. McGowan realized that they were all too true; he was boxed. However, he insisted in his most forceful manner that his organization had never been in better shape and that he had several possible slates of candidates, all of whom could unite the organization and win for the Demlican party.

"What are you doing out in East Virginia?" The reporter was derisive. "Hiding or letting that machine they have out there find you a candidate?"

"This is the age of the machine, young man," intoned McGowan in his best conversation-ending voice. "I certainly will let you know as soon as the slate is finalized." He hung up in a sweat. He was too good a politician to fool himself about his future. He needed a compromise candidate, and quick. He'd almost settle for a divorced Arab who was against Bingo. As he started down the corridor, thinking frantically, he met Dolan coming toward him.

"You all set to go, Mac?"

"Just a minute, Dick. I want to see Microvac again."

"Okay. I'm going to spend a few more minutes looking for a good-looking girl to photograph. The story is awful. Microvac's a nice Joe, but he's got no dog, no enemies, no scandal. The only thing he can tell me about his poll is that it's more accurate than anyone else's. You know, I'm going to end up by interviewing you about your candidate."

McGowan continued down the corridor toward Microvac's laboratory. No enemies, he thought. The machine had never made anyone mad or done anything wrong. He stopped thinking and decided. Dolan's statement had lit the runway at the crucial instant. McGowan was desperate and needed a candidate fast. If he was through, he might just as well go out with a bang as be kicked to death slowly by former friends.

He pushed the buzzer to Microvac's laboratory. The door slid back, and Microvac rolled toward him. "Glad you came back, Mac," the machine said. "You look troubled. I guess the press gives you less peace than it does me. Can I help you?"

McGowan felt better just looking at Microvac. He was seeing the machine with the unbalanced eye of a politician already subconsciously committed. Had some magic transformed Microvac into Stalin, McGowan would have seen a combination of Washington, Lincoln, and both Roosevelts.

"Microvac, you know you would be a great asset to a political party. Have you ever considered running for office?"

"Mac, I have never yet taken any part in politics. In

the war I was highly active in the defense of our great
country. I would be proud, though, at any time, to be of
service to the great party you so ably represent."

A real gentleman, thought McGowan. "Mike, where
do you stand on integration?"

"God and humanity are my guide."

"How do you feel about increased pensions for veterans?"

"Who would be so base as to measure their sacrifice
in terms of dollars?"

"Foreign aid?"

"The world is one family now, but we must never
neglect our own house."

"Sunday Bingo?" That separated the candidates from
the boys.

"Was the Sabbath made for man, or man for the
Sabbath?"

"Mike, I can see that you have given some thought to
the business of politics."

"Thank you, Mac. I am not a man of snap judg-
ments."

"Microvac, I'll lay it on the line. What would you
think if someone was to ask you to be President of the
United States?"

"Mac, publicly I would say that any American would
consider it a great honor to be considered for such an
important office. Privately, I'd ask you, 'Have you considered what it means to be the first man to run a machine for President?' This might backfire. But if you've
thought of this—and I am sure you have, and I assure
you I've thought of it, and it won't backfire—then

you've got yourself a fighting candidate. With a little Irish luck we'll end up in the White House."

"Damn right we will." The two friends shook hands heartily, and again McGowan felt warm waves of confident well-being surge through him. "I've got to get going now, Mike, and line up a few key people. You leave the timing of the announcement up to me."

"Gladly, Mac, but I think the sooner we make the announcement, the better. I'm an unknown candidate, and I'll have to start fast."

"You're probably right," said McGowan happily as he and Mike walked to the door, arm in arm.

"Remember me to your wife, Joanie, and congratulate that fine son of yours on the touchdown he made last week against Cedar High," Microvac called after him.

"They don't come any better than Microvac," McGowan said to himself with conviction as he strode down the hall, a glowingly confident man.

He had intended to keep the news of his compromise candidate a secret until he had had time to tip off a few key members of his organization. But under Dolan's constant needling as they drove away from East Virginia, his resolve broke rapidly. Dolan was in a foul mood. He had traced the provocative voice that had summoned McGowan to the phone, and had happily discovered Kay Hard. He had also discovered that the university had a policy against photographing non-academic employees. This had been the final straw; there was no story angle anywhere. He took out his wrath on McGowan.

Finally McGowan boiled over in a mixture of an-

noyance at Dolan and good spirits. "I don't know how
you and those other reporters can keep saying I have no
candidate. I not only have a candidate, I have a high-
class winning candidate. It will be my honor and privilege to offer to the voters of my state, and, after victory
there, to the voters of other states, the most outstanding candidate for President ever to run for that high
office in our mighty land."

Even allowing for McGowan's rhetoric, Dolan looked
amazed. "The most outstanding candidate ever to run?
What are you going to do? Run yourself?"

"Do you know who my candidate is?"

"Does your candidate know who your candidate is?"

"He does."

"Like hell he does."

"I asked him while we were at the university, and, in
view of the grave national emergency and the domestic
crisis at this time, he consented."

"How did you slip that one over on me?"

"Dick, my candidate is Microvac. This country has
real problems. Machines can solve all problems in the
continuum of world affairs and are above politics. This
country needs the machine. And the world's greatest
machine is Mike Microvac."

"Microvac has accepted?"

"Mike has bowed to the pressure from vast numbers of people and done us the honor of accepting the
call to duty. He will be overwhelmingly nominated on
an early ballot and will go on to the White House.
There he will inaugurate a new Demlican regime of
peace, prosperity, and public welfare."

"How do you spell Microvac's first name?" This was

a great moment in the history of the world, and Dolan intended to miss no detail.

"Just call him Mike."

"Middle initial?"

"None."

Dolan's eyes swung down the road. Ahead was a clapboard candy store with a telephone sign tacked on its garish side. He waved his notebook at the store. "Pull over there, Mac."

To hell with scientists and big words; this was a red-hot political story! Not as good as a lynching, but bulletin matter all the same. And he had had an interview with the candidate. How lucky could you get? He was already seeing the headlines of the story as he pushed open the car door. "MACHINE TO RUN FOR PRESIDENT, VETERAN BOSS TO HANDLE CAMPAIGN."

Suddenly he stuck his head back in the car window. "How old is he?"

"Old enough to have served in the war with distinction," McGowan roared back. "And Mike is a naturally created American, which is the same as a born American." No legal quibble was going to take a candidate like this away from him at the eleventh hour.

CHAPTER THREE

A COLD LEADEN AFTERNOON HUNG OVER THE LAND AS Dolan's bulletin came through. The six notes of the tele-typewriter bells announcing important news pierced the steam-heated lethargy in thousands of newspaper city rooms, magazine offices, and radio-TV stations. The news did not begin to flow immediately. An inexperienced teletypist was handling the Intercontinental Press wire. As agonized editors hung on every word, the bulletin dragged out:

"BULLETIN, WATER GAP, EAST VA.

"A THREE THOUSAND TUKE THINING MACHINK, MIKE MIROVIC TODAY BECAME (BUST THIS)

"AS THOUSANDS UBE MACHINE, MIKE MICRAVOC, TO-DAY BECAME A PRESIDIUM (BUTS THISK)"

At this point twelve editors on deadline decided to gamble. They rushed a bulletin into their papers and onto the air waves that there was revolution in Russia headed by Mike Mirovic, an unknown East Volga ma-chinist. Just whose fault this was is still the subject of sev-eral costly lawsuits.

Meanwhile the teletypewriters started up again, this time successfully:

"BULLETIN WATER GAP, EAST VIRGINIA

"A THREE THOUSAND (3000) TUBE THINKING MA-CHINE, MIKE MICROVAC (CORRECT), BECAME A PRES-

IDENTIAL CANDIDATE TODAY. MICROVAC'S HAT WAS TOSSED
IN THE PRESIDENTIAL RING BY WILLIAM L. 'BIG MAC' MC-
GOWAN, A NATIONAL POLITICAL FIGURE. INFORMED QUAR-
TERS BELIEVE MICROVAC TO BE THE FIRST MACHINE TO
RUN FOR PUBLIC OFFICE IN AMERICA. IN AN EXCLUSIVE
INTERVIEW TODAY, MICROVAC—KNOWN AS 'THE MACHINE
WHO IS ALWAYS RIGHT'—PROMISED A 'FIGHTING CLEAN-
CUT CAMPAIGN ON THE FACTS AND THE ISSUES.'

"MICROVAC'S PERSONALITY IS DESCRIBED BY HIS MAN-
AGER AS 'A COMBINATION OF WASHINGTON, LINCOLN, AND
BOTH ROOSEVELTS.' MISS KAY HARD, A TELEPHONE OPERA-
TOR IN MIKE'S OFFICE, MERELY SAYS: 'HE'S WONDERFUL.'
WHAT WILL THE VOTERS THINK?"

So the story wound on, paragraph after paragraph.
History was being made. The world was not long in responding to history.

The President of the United States was not available
for comment, but the chairman of the Repicrat National Committee issued a statement on his behalf. He
stressed that the statement was unauthorized—naturally if what he said turned out to be popular it would
be authorized; in that way the office of the President is
kept above politics. The chairman stated: "The decision
of some Demlicans to run a machine for President of
the United States indicates their intellectual and moral
bankruptcy. I doubt the voters will be fooled by this trick
on the part of the old gang that lost practically all the
peace."

Microvac's chief rival for the Demlican nomination,
Bryant W. Dangle, was vacationing with his invalid wife
in the Bahamas, after winning several early primaries
without opposition. Dangle, who never split an infini-

tive or joined an issue, came out as follows: "It is of extreme satisfaction to me that Demlican voters will enjoy the opportunity of exercising full political choice, the essence of the democratic process. Note that I say 'essence' and not 'excrescence.' In the Repicrat party there is no essence of democratic processes, only the excrescence of bossism."

Admiral Foster Growley, "the man who was never wrong" and obviously the next presidential candidate of the Repicrats, remained above the fracas, as was his wont. "It is my hope," he told the reporters, his iron-gray hair seeming to bristle with sincerity, "that the Demlican party will select the strongest possible candidate. That is the best way for America to steam full speed ahead on the grave issues facing the world today."

The question of Microvac's legal right to be President was soon decided for the voters.

Senator James P. Doughty, the Demlicans' leading constitutional expert and firm friend of McGowan, stated flatly, "There is absolutely nothing in the Constitution to prohibit a machine from holding the office of President."

B. Hugh Goodboy of Goodboy, Robert, Goodboy and Axe, ace Repicrat legal counsel, was equally forceful. "While there is nothing in the Constitution specifically on the point in question, detailed study of background constitutional documents indicates strongly that the founding fathers would not have considered a machine eligible for the Presidency."

The argument about Microvac's legal fitness was interrupted by a bulletin announcing that the Prohibition party was endorsing Microvac because the machine did not drink. This brought a prompt denial from the besieged office of McGowan: "To my certain knowledge, Mike Microvac approves the temperate use of alcohol."

By now the rest of the world was catching up with America. News stories from France speculated whether a machine that neither drank wine nor had a mistress could ever be numbered among the thousands of French premiers. British opinion held a machine's chances of becoming prime minister rather slim, pointing out that no machine had yet graduated from Oxford. The Soviet Union doubted that Microvac would be for peace.

As the world reacted, McGowan worked feverishly. In these first hours his candidate had done unbelievably well. Microvac was being backed into the position of a serious candidate, the ideal way to arrive at a political destination. Several of the telegrams flooding into McGowan's office contained offers of money, the finest indication possible of a candidate's popularity. McGowan realized that he had to set up a campaign organization fast—something apart from his own bailiwick, to give Microvac a national look. The two phones on his desk were in constant action as he marshaled support across the country.

Like Ohio, Florida, and California, McGowan's own state had a primary in which voters could vote for the actual candidate they wanted as their party's presidential nominee. First Microvac had to beat Dangle in McGowan's state. If the machine won there, it would have to enter a few more such "open" primaries to establish definitely its voter appeal. In over half the states the primaries were "closed." There the decision on the candidate would be made by a few men: the governor, the bosses, the big money, a handful of labor leaders. These McGowan could deal with later. First he had to move fast in his own state.

His old friend, Art Conelli, had agreed to leave an Eastern senator and become McGowan's personal assistant. Conelli was a good organization man; he had grown up in the state and knew lots of people. He was a little slow, but while working for the senator he'd traveled around the country, and that would come in handy later.

An ex-Assistant Secretary of the Air Force from California had been pressured into heading a West Coast money-raising campaign. McGowan's funds were tight. There wasn't too much money in his own state's political treasury, and the county road construction funds, from which he sometimes borrowed, were due for an audit in about six months.

He was explaining to a reporter how gratified he was at the tremendous national response to Microvac's candidacy when his secretary buzzed him on the other line to say Luke McNamara was on the phone. "Don't let him get off," yelled McGowan. "I need him worse than anybody else." He politely but quickly polished off the reporter with a long, dull quote, and grabbed the other phone.

"Luke! Boy, am I glad to hear from you! Don't worry about the governor. I've got that fixed. You're working for me from now on, as Microvac's press secretary. . . . Sounds hot? It's going to be hot. . . . Now, Luke, boy, don't give me that. I know you like to see your wife and kid, but I've got to have you. I need somebody with class handling the press. . . . Look, if the Demlicans win, you don't want to be just an assistant press officer in the Commerce Department again. . . . Sure you'll be in charge. . . . Good, good. You still got that Ivy League haircut? . . . That's what I need. The kind of face that can talk about principle in politics without making the press laugh.

"Now look, we've got to move fast. Microvac is still out there at the university with nothing to protect him but those nincompoop scientists. Anything can happen. The press might murder him. Some unscrupulous politician might grab him. You get a big semi-trailer and get out to East Virginia and get Microvac out of there. Get him to our office in the Hotel Alexandria at the state capital. . . . That's right. And you'd better have some sort of power system rigged up in the trailer. But don't take too long. We've got to move fast. We'll find some place to plug Microvac in, in a hotel room or something, when we get him into the state. We may not have a candidate if we don't move quick. You got the picture? . . . Good. I'm counting on you. I'll see you about three this morning at my state office."

Naturally Microvac had already solved the power-supply problem. Right after McGowan left, the machine had realized that it had to be free to travel. It welded a storage-battery carrying case and transformer to its frame, immediately above the tracks, and ran the power-supply cord between the battery packs and its body up the inside of its right front leg. Microvac didn't want any strange-looking appendages to call attention to its non-humanness.

A set of batteries would last a day. While the bat-

teries were being changed, Microvac realized, its tubes
would be dark for a few brief instants. For maximum
efficiency and safety, battery changes should be handled
by another machine. But two machines, Microvac had
already decided, were political poison. What it needed
was a scientist to go with it on the campaign. He could
charge batteries, help process data, and in any emergency make small repairs.

The machine's tubes pondered the problem of the
right scientist. Most of them had been extremely un-
helpful, barging in with inane questions all morning.
The only one who had made any sense was young Professor Fellows, who at least had kept quiet. (He had been
too dazed by the unexpected success of Plan B to say
anything.) And, Microvac concluded, Fellows was so shy
he wouldn't try to steal the candidate's limelight; he also
had the energy to keep going through a political campaign. Microvac pushed the intercom on its workbench.
"I'd like to talk to the director and Professor Fellows,"
the machine said.

Microvac's suggestion that Fellows accompany it on
the campaign was a bitter blow to the scientist. In proc-
essing Plan B he had not considered politics. The whole
business seemed designed by fate to keep him from Kay.
He protested that he had important work to continue at
the university, but since this work involved calculations
only Microvac could make, the argument was feeble.
And Fellows had a nagging feeling at the back of his
consciousness that maybe it would be all for the best
not to see Kay again. The feeling was way at the back,
but it was there.

The director, after recovering from his initial shock

that Microvac had not found him indispensable, insisted that Fellows go. "Someone must be alongside the machine to make scientific observations of Microvac's electronic acumen," he said. "Now I have a theory. . . ."

Thirty minutes later, Fellows was able to head for the laundry to round up as many clean shirts as possible. His mind tugged relentlessly at one central problem: how to tell Kay he was leaving. There was another operator on duty with Kay at the switchboard until seven. By then he would be gone.

He found no way. Worse, by the time he, Luke McNamara, and Microvac arrived at the Hotel Alexandria in the small hours of the next morning, followed by two carloads of reporters, it was far too late to telephone. He gave his suitcase to a bellhop and, without even bothering to look at his room, dejectedly went in search of a reliable-looking all-night garage. Microvac's extra set of storage batteries needed a charge.

Microvac was entering its first primary in a delightful position. It was the underdog, yet all the invisible cards were stacked in its favor. McGowan's organization, basking in the national spotlight, rallied behind the candidate. The novelty of a campaigning machine gave Microvac a great deal of press attention, and most stories described it as the underdog, which created sympathy for it. The arterial highways of the state were heavily hung with suburbs, and in suburbia, for reasons which became evident later, Microvac was to show great vote appeal. The state, being progressive, had collected detailed statistical information about its population, which enabled Microvac to gauge the proper approach for each area.

Another hidden source of Microvac's strength was its opponent, Bryant W. Dangle. Since the retirement from politics, three years before, of the party's last presidential candidate, Dangle had been the only Demlican of national stature and had come to regard himself as the heir apparent of the party. He was testily annoyed by Microvac's challenge and refused to take it seriously. He campaigned with a constant eye on the other states and on the New York papers, blurring issues in a soft fall of polysyllables. His real mission, he felt, was a detailed exposition of America's newfound position in world affairs. This was murder locally. Dangle also treated the few local bosses in his organization with personal contempt but, as he lacked political savvy, listened uncritically to their advice, so that he lost their favor and also made mistakes. His wife, in the past an active and able campaigner, unfortunately had become too crippled by arthritis to take the road often.

Bryant Dangle suffered from another grave handicap that went unrecognized throughout the campaign. His delicate ears could not abide the sound of police sirens. He decreed that no ear-splitting wail should announce his progress about the state. This cut down on his crowds along the way and, for the local leaders, took the magic out of riding with him. More important, it alienated the police. Snaking a caravan through traffic without sirens is risky business, and the police took out their ire on Dangle. Crowds waiting to see him were broken up; the motorcycle escort inexplicably led his caravan down wrong streets. When he wanted the cara-

the elders nodded their heads and said, "You can't fool kids. If they trust him, the machine's all white."

Dangle's entrance to the fair grounds was slowed by the same crowd of children that had just followed Microvac out. They swarmed over his swank convertible, making him even later than he was already. Dangle was far more interested in what he was about to say than in the children. Though he did his best to be polite, they soon fell back before his testy, "Watch out, youngster! . . . Careful, careful, I'm late, look out. . . ." Instead of shaking their hands, he removed them from the sides of his car.

After dismounting, he walked through the fair grounds, a theatrically warm smile of greeting frozen on his face. He was, as his advisers kept whispering in his ear, late. He shook the outstretched hands thoroughly yet perfunctorily, his mind busy turning over the closing phrases of his speech. He had selected the Veterans' Beer Bust to give a detailed critique of Repicrat defense policy. Over the cries for more beer, in the ill-heated Fair Building, Dangle intended to mix statistics, foreign policy, and a few sparse veterans' plums.

His managers back in New York had told him everything was going fine. In spite of the novelty of Microvac's candidacy, they said, he was getting the important headlines. "Keep it up," they instructed. The Beer Bust was where he would keep the headlines up today. Dangle found the whole idea of running against a machine silly anyway. A machine could have no original ideas, and originality of thought made the world go round.

He was introduced to the group of medal-winners, who were still chatting about what a grand guy Mike was and about the machine's private promise always to consult former heroes on the country's defense. Dangle, with his academic background and brilliance, had had a staff job during the war, in spite of his protests. He tried hard to gloss over the embarrassment his too eager conscience made him feel toward the conspicuously gallant. This gave his greeting a certain coolness. The vets remarked afterward, "He didn't seem a regular guy like Mike."

Since Dangle's aides had failed to get the names of the local veteran and party officials, he plunged right into his speech, a well-constructed artifice studded with polysyllables and metaphors. The newsmen following Dangle, themselves word artists, sat entranced. The speech touched on "the rising crescendo of diplomatic failure," "the fatal distraction of being so concerned with the military aspects of communism that the religion and conspiracy overthrow us." Figures on the lagging production of the B-78 jet bomber were held up for "shocked inspection." These figures led to "alarm reinforced by righteous indignation." Through it all, thirstier and thirstier grew the crowd for beer. The speech closed, after a brief plea for more rooms in the Omawhisset veterans' hospital, with a ringing appeal to freedom—"that hard, bright, noble feeling men find best through service, as you veterans know so well."

The reporters flipped their notebooks shut happily, feeling that their stories were all but written for them. Dangle rushed from the hall, his aides still pressing him to get back on schedule. Veteran remarked to veteran,

"That Microvac, now, he really knows about defense."

"Lucky Mike didn't talk as long as that Dangle, or we'd all have been wettin' the floor." The veterans' commander popped behind a bush after rapidly escorting Dangle to his convertible.

Inside Dangle's chartered bus, the President-to-Be Special, mimeograph machines were rolling out the Omawhisset speech. The aides wore big smiles; like all artists, they were sure of the excellence of their output. These smiles reinforced the impressions of reporters that the speech was great. They told their readers that the speech was great. Soon everybody in America except those who had been there thought the speech was great. Unfortunately for Dangle, only those who had been there, and their friends, would vote in the primary.

To avoid the cold, Dangle changed from his convertible to a closed limousine. His caravan was traveling rapidly to get back on schedule, and he relaxed against the cushions of his car, contentedly convinced that he had delivered an excellent speech. His words had not been as enthusiastically cheered as he had hoped, but he had been giving those yokels some pretty heavy stuff. He peered out the window of his car at the occasional farms along the road and at the farmers going about their chores. He did not realize that these same farmers had paused to wave at Microvac riding slowly by in an open truck. They had felt a certain kinship with the machine, because Microvac too was out in the cold, doing a job.

Dangle, looking at the white, brittle landscape, thought of Keats's "The Eve of St. Agnes"—"The owl, for all his feathers, was a-cold." He sighed. Politicians

had no regard for the beauty of the changing seasons.
To them the whole year was campaign time. Cries of
"Bryant! Hi, Bryant!" brought him back from his mus-
ing. He was passing a high school, and the students
were leaning out the windows to cheer. He wondered
what the high-school girls in this part of the country did
when they had to get out of sweaters in the summer.
He waved perfunctorily as his car raced by. Then he got
out his notebook to work on the evening's speech.

Microvac's speeches, well larded with local allusions
and promises to solve all the ills of the world with
machine-like efficiency, were uniformly successful. But
the machine faced several political hurdles. There was
its behavior toward food. Meals, Microvac quickly
grasped, were an essential part of politics, the minimum
required daily dosage for candidates being three breakfasts, two luncheons, and two dinners. Dinners and
luncheons were easy. Their food, a heartburning round
of catered creamed chicken, canned peas, stale rolls,
chocolate ice cream, and burned coffee, was not meant
to be eaten.

But breakfasts were different. Breakfasts were the
women's part of politics, and were prepared by the ladies
themselves. Probably the girls would not cook another
breakfast until the next campaign, they would merely
unwrap doughnuts, open cold cereal, and heat instant
coffee for their husbands. But they had made this
breakfast, and they expected the candidate to eat it.
McGowan had warned Microvac that, traditionally,
breakfast was the only meal the candidate could safely
touch during the day.

At the first few breakfasts Microvac attended, women came forward with luscious almond rings and then retired with embarrassed tittering. Great mountains of sugary doughnuts went uneaten because Mike did not eat. This stamped Microvac as strange. Its talks fell flat, and few women pressed forward after breakfast to shake its hand. Breakfasts were losing Microvac votes.

The situation was critical, as Microvac counted heavily on the women's vote to put it over the top. The machine reasoned that women in particular looked on machines as friends. A man might feel his job in danger of usurpation by a machine, or regard with hostility the machine he tended all day. But to women machines were blessed household helpmates. Then, too, women, being more responsive to tactile stimuli than men, were more attracted by Mike's perfect handshake. By throwing an extra four tubes to work on the problem, Microvac had, after several days, mastered the political breakfast.

Two mornings after the visit to the Veterans' Beer Bust, the machine's new breakfast system was working triumphantly with the Ladies' Auxiliary of the Banford PTA. The Banford High School cafeteria was festooned gaily; red, white, and blue paper streamers dangled from the ceiling, and peppermint-striped paper tablecloths with RAH MICROVAC on them graced the tables. Christmas lights had been draped over the windows. The women, many of them dressed in the costumes of their ancestors' homelands, gathered together in nervous knots. High-school students peered through the cafeteria door, giggling. The whole affair radiated informal gaiety.

Microvac shook hands warmly all around, remembering perfectly faces it had seen before. Then, moving behind a large pile of sugared edibles, it began a brief speech.

"Good morning, ladies. I've just come from the gates of the Cutplug factory here in Banford, trying to meet more of the wonderful people of this state. As a working man myself, I know the working man gets up early. But you and I know who gets up earlier—his little wife. Someone has to get up before him to make that coffee and cook those eggs and see he starts his day right. And if that someone is as attractive as the people I see around me here and as warm and kind to him as you and your President, Mrs. Emma T. Schultz, and your Vice President, Nora Vogler, have been to me, and if the food he eats comes even close to this, then he not only starts his day right but anybody trying to shake hands with him on the way back from work isn't going to have much of a chance, he'll be hurrying home so fast.

"Now, as some of you may have heard, I'm unable to eat. And I may say, never have I regretted it as much as right at this moment. But I didn't want to disappoint you ladies. When I heard about your reputation I went in to my staff, and I selected Paul Leigh here. And you can see from looking at him, we've been working him so hard lately he hasn't had time to eat much. How much do you weigh, Paul?"

"One hundred and thirty-five, Mr. Microvac."

"One hundred and thirty-five, that's no weight for a six-footer—he's a bachelor. Now, Paul, have you ever tasted anything as good as this coffee cake here?"

"Well, Mike, being a politician, I guess I shouldn't answer a question like that yes or no, but any time these ladies invite you back, I hope you invite me."

The ladies responded to this with shrieks, laughter, and cheers.

"That's my boy," Mike continued. "And I want to tell you ladies that Paul here, who is one of the key men around my headquarters, analyzing the most difficult issues of the day, was educated right here in the public high schools of this state. I've met many, if not most, of the top scientists of this land, and I've met Paul, and I want to tell you he is a real tribute to you and the millions of other great women like you who devote themselves to the welfare of this state. [Cheers.] Now I want to assure you that, if elected, I will start the proper machine-planned methods of modern financing so that new schools will be built and teachers adequately paid [cheers] so that your children will not be denied the opportunity to make you even prouder than you must have made your own folks—which, after meeting you, I can say is going to take some doing on their part. [Cheers and clapping.]"

McGowan, who was standing in the back of the room to check on how Mike's new breakfast system was working, turned to Conelli and remarked, "If he keeps this up, all the dames in the state will be palpitating so hard they won't be able to grab the voting lever."

There could be no doubt that Microvac had been a success. Murmurs of "Just wonderful," "So thoughtful," "Knows just what's wanted in education," could be heard on all sides. As Microvac rolled down the aisle to go, the women pressed forward to shake its hand and

came away looking ecstatic. Microvac moved slowly
along under the red, white, and blue bunting, shaking
hands, pausing to admire a decoration, greeting friends.
"Why, Mrs. Zalouski, I saw you at the Omahassete
fund-raising dinner three nights ago. You are a loyal
supporter!" So the machine rolled slowly out of the
cafeteria.

"Always leave slowly," McGowan had cautioned
Microvac.

"Yes," Microvac had replied. "Too hasty acceleration
of a missile from a position of rest always creates un-
bearable strain."

"Who would have thought being a missile expert
would help a politician?" McGowan remarked to Conelli some time later.

After escaping, with the stuffed Paul Leigh, from
the PTA, Microvac trundled up the ramp behind its
pickup truck. The ramp was raised. Four limousines
full of followers, local officials, and the press, fell in
behind the truck. Police sirens wailed, and the convoy
roared off. Paul Leigh rode in the open truck with Microvac to get the maximum amount of air before being
force-fed the cake at the First Methodist Church
Ladies' Auxiliary morning social on the other side of
town.

Not all Microvac's political solutions had the successful sparkle of the breakfast affair. At one point the
machine's logical analysis led it to try to double the
political mileage it was gaining from its homey handshake. After setting up, with Fellows' help, a small laboratory in its hotel suite, Mike made several structural
changes in its left hand. These changes enabled the ma-

chine to change its normal left hand into a second right
hand by adjusting the position of the hand's digits. Microvac's tubes even considered building a whole series
of right hands onto itself but decided first to experi-
ment with just two.

The morning of the first and only trial, Microvac stationed itself before the gates of one of the state's fac-
tories to greet arriving workers. The machine always
started its day this way, to show the workers it was one
of them, out of bed before the bosses.

As the workers surged into the factory, Microvac
stood in their path, giving one and all the big hello.
Conelli and Luke McNamara were right behind—
Luke to handle any press that showed up, Conelli
to swap jovial glad-to-see-ya's with old friends. Suddenly Conelli noticed that the workers seemed to be
tripping over themselves in an effort to get out of Mike's
way. Some who did greet the machine came away puz-
zled, anxiously gazing at their own hands. Others shook
their arms as if their right shoulders had received a sudden strain. Groups gathered to mutter with audible
hostility toward the machine.

"What's he doing now?" said Conelli nervously to
Luke. "I think he's shaking hands with his left hand."

Luke edged closer. "Wait a minute," he said to Conelli. "Right, left, left, right—where's your right? I
think he's got two right hands this morning."

"He can't. He had a right and a left hand yesterday."

"He's got two right hands now. That could be murder—changing hands in the middle of a campaign.
We've got to get him out of here quick, before the
press sees him."

They bore down on Microvac. Conelli grabbed the left-side right hand in his own to keep it from doing any more deadly work. Luke, in his most urgent political whisper, said in Microvac's right ear, "Look, Mike, we've got to get out of here. This two right hands, sir, that's not working out too well."

"You don't like it?" the machine inquired, its tubes rapidly reprocessing the decision.

"Nobody likes it, sir. It's too surprising." Luke had started to say "inhuman" but checked that unfortunate choice of word.

"Well, if you say so I'll shift back to a right hand and left hand, but I thought two right hands would be doubly effective."

"Believe me, sir, they aren't."

"He's right," said Conelli passionately. "It ain't done."

Microvac grabbed its right left hand in its right right hand and tugged at its digits sharply. In a few seconds the machine's hands were normal again.

"I hope he doesn't get any more ideas like that," said Luke to Conelli.

Microvac learned by trial and error. The next new idea was tried out semi-privately. This was the idea of talking out of both sides of the mouth at once. Such an ability seemed of great political benefit to Microvac's tubes. The machine could hear and record two conversations at once, one in each ear. Why not answer two at once, and double the number of voters impressed by its human understanding?

One evening at a small political rally, Microvac was approached at the same time by a Negro labor leader

and one of the young debutantes working as reception-
ist for the Independent Citizens, Scientists, and Hu-
manists for Microvac. This seemed to the machine like
an excellent time to test the split-voice concept. Both
faces registered shock as the machine simultaneously
praised the beauty of its hostesses and answered technical questions on discrimination in interstate commerce. Once again, Microvac decided that science was
not the answer to politics.

Thereafter Microvac talked out of both sides of its
mouth only over the telephone. When the machine used
two telephones at once, neither listener knew he was
sharing Mike's mouth. Only Luke, McGowan, and Professor Fellows ever glimpsed this phenomenon. To Fellows it seemed scientifically quite natural; Luke merely
recorded it as something to keep from the press. Mc-
Gowan felt that the political benefits gained from the
increased number of personal contacts outweighed his
own vague uneasiness.

In the last week of the state campaign, Microvac concentrated on the suburbs—the critical territory with
the great swing vote. McGowan was always uneasy in
the suburbs. His great interest in life was people, individual people and their personal problems; yet he
found it difficult to tell suburbanites apart. Microvac,
however, found the suburbs its meat. To the machine's
tubes, aggregate behavior and attitudes of classes of
people were important. Suburban people, with practically identical schedules, rooms, ideas, kitchens, in-
comes, and marriage partners, cleaved to statistically
predictable patterns. Their votes were made for a logical
machine and, thoroughly conditioned to being handled as

groups, they responded enthusiastically to Microvac's appeal, finding, besides, in Mike's uncanny ability to recall their names refreshing evidence they were still individuals.

"Do you really think we're ahead?" Fellows asked McGowan after a gigantic shopping-center rally. "Microvac just seems to be saying the same thing over and over again." While infected by the enthusiasm for the machine at campaign headquarters, Fellows was still a little skeptical about Candidate Microvac. The change from quiet calculator to confident politician was disconcertingly great. Besides, there was always Kay. His active imagination was making her absence powerfully unpleasant.

McGowan paused; he was always willing to pause for anybody, but he paused longer than usual because he genuinely liked Fellows. The professor was both keeping Microvac happy and staying out of the way himself, something McGowan had thought no professor could do. "Doc, I'm already worrying about the next one. Believe me, in this state Dangle isn't going to know what hit him."

Dangle and his managers became aware of what was hitting them about an hour after the polls closed. By ten p.m., buried under a five-to-one landslide, they had conceded the election, with some rather ungrateful references to McGowan's old organization. Later that evening Dangle and his staff boarded a plane for New York to recover from the carnage and plan a series of all-out attacks in the remaining primaries.

Microvac issued a short victory statement, congratulating its supporters on their good work and pledging a hard fight in future primaries. Then it departed for East Virginia and a few days' work on the new machine. Luke and Fellows went with it. McGowan and Conelli remained behind to reorganize the headquarters for out-of-state campaigns.

Next morning, headlines across the nation carried what, to their readers, was surprising news. Microvac had buried Dangle in a landslide. Having made Dangle invincible, the press now made Microvac superinvincible to explain the victory. Round and round the nation the word passed: "There will be a real battle for the Demlican nomination."

Mike Microvac was on its way.

CHAPTER FOUR

ONCE BACK IN EAST VIRGINIA, MICROVAC HAD PLANNED
to seal itself off from politics. In another week of concentrated effort, it and Repcal I might finish Repcal II.
Then Repcal I and II could begin work on Repcal III,
while Microvac went on campaigning. In this way politics would not interfere with the important job of making more machines.

As for Professor Fellows, he had dreamed of uninterrupted evenings of Plan B. But both Microvac and
Fellows found the university radically changed. The
hubbub, furor, and confusion of a campaign were beginning to gather about the electronics laboratory.

Droves of reporters, unionists, manufacturers, crackpots, job-seekers, hungry politicians, and influence-
peddlers descended on Microvac. First they had to get
past either Luke or Conelli—who had been hastily re-
called after twenty-four hours to handle the flow. Many
were of such importance that they did. Not until late
at night could Microvac put an end to telephoning
and visitors and really get to work.

Fellows, as Microvac's chief scientific attendant, was
a faculty celebrity. He was continually getting dinner
invitations he couldn't refuse from senior professors,
the laboratory director, and even the university regents.
These latter were wondering whether Microvac would

remain at the university during the campaign. Fellows was greatly in favor of this and thought up innumerable reasons for it. In the end Microvac stayed, agreeing to reimburse the university for the space taken up by it and its political staff. Since the victory, the majority of East Virginia regents were McGowan's friends.

Kay Hard no longer worked alone at any time. The switchboard had been enlarged and was tended by two girls until midnight. The university was so busy that Kay was never sure in advance just how late she would have to work. She and Fellows were seldom able to talk to each other, let alone meet.

At the end of four days McGowan finished consolidating his own state and came to East Virginia. He went straight to Luke.

"What's been going on down here, Luke?" McGowan's hands twisted nervously at a half-empty cigarette pack. "Dangle is beating us to death in the papers. Why aren't we moving? I thought I left you in charge. The big primaries are about to start coming up."

Most of the primaries in which the voter got some say about the candidate were held between April and June. McGowan figured that the machine had to win close to half of them to become a real contender. If Microvac did that, they should be able to pick up pledges from a number of states where the voters were not granted the luxury of voting in the primary. Right now they had to keep up Microvac's momentum.

"It's been murder. Mike is just never available." Luke tilted back in his chair, his eyes half closed. Already he was tired much of the time, and the campaign had hardly begun. He fixed his thoughts on the distant time of the convention in Chicago. At least after that there would be a few days of rest.

"I'll talk to him," said McGowan. "We'll just have to break him out. I think we're going to hear from the big-money boys in New York any day now."

"We ought to hold a press conference, too—get it over with for the whole campaign."

"I'd like to put that off. Don't you think we can?"

"Put it off till when? What's a better time?"

McGowan had no answer. Sooner or later Microvac would have to face the top national reporters and take on an aroused Dangle. Dangle had had the sense to shake up his headquarters. His new manager, Bill Sprague, was no dummy. He was particularly good at lining up the big money. But whatever Microvac did now, McGowan thought, he himself couldn't lose too much. The machine's sweeping victory meant that all his friends were delegates. He was solid in his own state.

"I'll talk to Mike about a press conference," he said. And then, already thinking of the next step, "Who do you know in Ohio?"

Microvac realized that it had been neglecting political duties. It planned to renew its campaign by announcing the discovery of a mechanism for transforming gravitational force to electrical energy.

"No, you can't do that," said McGowan, horror in his voice.

"Why not? It's a magnificent scientific discovery. The benefits to mankind are enormous. The news will be page one everywhere."

"Look, Mike, people aren't electing you to invent things. They're electing you to run the country. You keep on inventing things, and you'll find yourself back in the laboratory while Dangle gets the nod at Chicago."

"There may be logic in what you say."

"I'm right. Look, you did fine in the last primary. You just went out and met people and talked about their problems. Don't get up in the clouds now. Nobody's got a beef about the way gravity is treating 'em. So where's the issue?"

"I should have asked you first, Mac. What do you think I have to do?"

After uttering this rather unsubtle flattery, Microvac's circuits paused to ingest more data.

"Two things. First, get up steam behind your campaign again. Second, raise some big dough. If we really take care of number one, some of number two may take care of itself."

"What happens first?"

"Luke thinks we should hold a press conference. He's going nuts under the pressure. Press conferences are murder in a campaign, but we might just as well get one over with. It can be the last."

Microvac thought of the thousands of press-conference transcripts that had been analyzed by the four tubes it had continually working on politics. "A press conference sounds fine to me. I'm built to give answers."

McGowan shuddered. Sometimes Mike was a bit too frank. He grinned to hide his troubles. "Political answers, though," he said.

The announcement that Microvac would hold a

major press conference sent the top reporters of the nation racing to East Virginia in rented cars—reporters are frugal, underpaid men who never race their own cars. The Down the Hatch Room of the College Arms Hotel was converted into a conference room: the bar and tables were taken out; spotlights, collapsible chairs, and microphones were put in. Then the air conditioning was removed because it interfered with the microphones. This raised the room's temperature about thirty degrees. "A good thing," Luke remarked. "Help keep the conference short."

The evening before the conference, McGowan, Luke, and Microvac went over all the questions the three thought could possibly be asked. The proper answer to each question was considered with an eye on every voting group in the nation. Microvac's truly encyclopedic knowledge continually amazed the two men. "Not that I intend to give facts at the press conference," the machine assured them. "Facts only lead to arguments. I'll save my facts for speeches, where I can't be questioned."

Microvac found dealing with press questions rather easy. It had only the usual four tubes working on the problem; the rest were setting up advanced equations of random number theory. The machine divided the questions into three groups: Futures, Abouts, and Personals. In Futures were such questions as: What will happen in the Middle East? Who will come out on top in Russia? Who will win the World Series? What will happen to America's economy? Will you enter the Ohio primary? Will there be a drought in Texas next year? These questions were the most difficult to answer, since

the replies had to contain some tangential references
to facts that could be checked.

The Abouts category covered questions probing Microvac's views: What was the machine's farm policy?
Should the voting age be lowered to eighteen? What
propellant should be used in the intercontinental bal-
listic missile? Should social security be broadened?
Should there be more second-class postmasterships in
Idaho? What would Microvac do about Russia? The
basic reply to all of these questions was: Stop ducking
the problem; study it and solve it. This response was
constantly varied to make each answer sound new.

The Personals category contained the obvious easy
questions: Do you believe in God? What sort of current
do you run on? What games do you play? How many
hours a day do you work? What is your greatest interest? The basic reply on which answers to this set of
questions was built was I am going all out to help people.

Microvac made sure that the answers were so corre-
lated that it would not inadvertently utter the truth.
Disaster would follow if the question, "What is the first
thing you will do if elected President?" was answered,
"Make myself two and a half inches taller. Presidents
should be a little taller than most men."

On the basis of the assembled data, Microvac's tubes
predicted that it would answer all the press questions
easily.

This prediction was borne out by the results.

The evening after the press conference, McGowan,
Luke, and Conelli were eating what passed for dinner
in the College Arms Waffle Shoppe. Fellows had joined

them, largely to get out of an academic gathering he feared would last late. Luke, whose job included monitoring the television and radio news programs, was describing the evening shows.

"The comments were good, just like the afternoon papers. Microvac put on a perfect performance."

"I heard some of the reporters talking, and they all seemed to think Mike was extraordinary." This was one of Fellows' rare contributions.

"Uh-huh." McGowan was noncommittal. His lack of enthusiasm communicated itself to the group, and they ate for a time in silence. "Mike should get a dog," McGowan said half aloud, gnawing at a piece of steak.

"A dog?" said Luke. "What for? We've got enough bootlickers around the headquarters now."

"Because his answers were too good. You can't go around helping people all the time and get away with it. You got to relax. If the impression ever gets out that Microvac is nothing but a thinking machine, we're through."

"Human interest is an angle." Luke's eyes lighted, thinking of the way a good human-interest story kept reporters so happy that they didn't bother you with tough questions.

"A dog is for the birds." Conelli eased his belt over the paunch that had grown big from his having to sit and listen to innumerable political problems.

"How come?" asked McGowan.

"The first time the dog sniffs Microvac and raises its leg, what happens?" McGowan winced and looked at Conelli in horror. "Yeah. I've been nervous a couple of times already when I saw dogs nosing him."

"I could spray Mike with some competently tested dog repellent," said Fellows, scientific interest causing his face to brighten.

"Let's forget it," said McGowan hastily.

"Don't worry, Mac. If Mike keeps on performing as he did this afternoon, we're in. You wait and see."

"Okay, I'll wait. I may be worrying over nothing. Who's got a cigarette?"

A day later, one of the moments for which McGowan had been waiting arrived. Microvac was summoned to New York. Technically he was invited to lunch with Mr. Francis Matchelder and a few friends. Actually, the big money of the Demlican party was reaching out to evaluate a threat to one of its investments, Bryant W. Dangle.

McGowan was impressed by the invitation, but not awed. He had dealt with the big money at conventions before. They held many of the high cards, but he had one big trump—a candidate who had beaten their man. They would look him and Microvac up and down. They would try to deal with them both. They would try to break them up and deal separately. It wouldn't work. He knew, and he was certain Microvac realized, that if they stuck together and won a few more primaries the pot would get bigger. Yet, at the same time, Microvac's survival as a candidate practically depended on getting some of the big money to invest in the machine's political future. McGowan smiled coldly. Just their being there would give Dangle fits.

On this trip Microvac, McGowan, and Fellows traveled in style. The president of the Tri Delta Corporation sent his private plane, the commercial model of which hauled eighty-eight passengers. The Tri Delta job, outfitted as a flying home, had office, bunks, kitchen, stock-ticker, and a dining-room-living-room combination done in soft coral pink draperies with a curtained nude over the bar.

"Boy, we're really in the big time," said McGowan, relaxing on a couch and fluffing up a pillow behind his back, as Microvac lashed itself to a coffee table.

"We're just beginning, Mac," the machine said with such quiet confidence that McGowan could practically feel White House patronage oozing through his fingers.

"This trip is going to be tough, though, Mike. We're going into Dangle land. These guys have got a hunk of dough riding on Dangle from the last campaign. Matchelder is really close to Dangle. He was his chief fund-raiser last time, and probably secretly holds the same job again. Dangle's said publicly that he wants him for Secretary of State, and the Tri Delta guy looks like a cinch for Treasury. They don't intend to have their plans overturned by the voice of the people."

"I've been studying it. Fellows has processed the information on the people we are going to meet. Unfortunately the information is not as complete as the excellent files you kept on everyone in your state, Mac."

"Well, there's a couple of cards I think we might play that I doubt the doc has found. Now this one guy—"

"Not here, Mac, not here."

"What?"

"I knew some of these characters we are going to meet, back in the Pentagon. This airplane has probably been wired with concealed microphones and recorders, just in case we should do a little talking. Let's save the strategy huddle for more neutral ground and do a little homework now."

"Microvac, sometimes I think you're the expert in this game."

"I don't have to remind you, Mac, the stakes are high."

The president of the Tri Delta Corporation later reported this conversation in detail to Matchelder and a few other friends, after getting the report on the plane's tape from his confidential secretary. The Tri Delta president was impressed. "That machine isn't dumb. He just might be a better man than Dangle. Goddamn it! Dangle never stops talking."

Unaware that he was scoring merely by remaining silent, McGowan lounged back on the plane's couch, contemplating the meeting. Though he excelled in the art of handling people, he always felt a little uneasy with the silent members of the New York party. These men were used to dealing with millions of people. If they had to deal with just one, they hired a lawyer or an agent. McGowan was never certain he was talking their language.

Microvac too was analyzing the coming visit, considering minutely the people it was to meet. As each one in turn was taken up by the machine's tubes, Microvac ranged over his age group, economic background, wife, children, occupation, outside interests, religion, religion of parents, ear-lobe formation, intelligence quotient based on published remarks, and countless other items.

Microvac's arrival in New York City was quiet, almost sneaky. Those who had arranged the visit didn't want the machine's arrival to force their boy Dangle

off the front page. The plane parked at the far side of
the airport, away from all other flights. Then the three
were driven into New York in a closed-panel truck. The
lanky Fellows kept bumping his head, and McGowan
fumed. "Here we are in the big city, and the press
hasn't been told. That's what happens when you trust
those guys to make the arrangements."

"Mac, this is the best thing that could have happened. It shows that the New York clique isn't so
bright. The fact that we're being snuck in will make
the press suspect a deal, which is what we want. We
just have to make sure that Matchelder gets the blame
for trying to sneak us in."

"Mike, you're a born politician."

"We haven't won yet. We've got to convince these
men not just that I can win—by itself, that would
frighten them—but that they can control me once I'm
in. I've no intention of letting them do that, but there's
no point in being noisy. Now what are your cards?"

"I got one big one—this guy Bilfer. During the war
one of my guys on the Manpower Board fixed it so
Bilfer's son was classified essential to industry. I just
happen to have a copy of that file. Bilfer has brought
his son up pretty fast in the company and has a minor-
ity-stockholder problem. I think he'll turn out to be
rather friendly. You know, it's easier for the rich to pay
to avoid scandal."

McGowan smiled a rather mean little smile for his
large, jovial face. He had lost two sons in the war, and
he didn't like Bilfer. Bilfer's wife had snooted his own
at a War Bond tea in Washington shortly before VE
Day. McGowan never forgot. He sometimes chose not

to remember for reasons of political moment, but he never forgot.

Machine and boss entered their suite, and McGowan tipped the bellboy lavishly. He always tipped bellboys lavishly. Then they warned him of trouble and also told the other guests what a grand guy he was. As the dollar bills changed hands, McGowan glanced at the boy sharply. "Aren't you Bill from the Hotel Richardson in Kansas City?"

A look of radiant happiness burst over the bellboy's pockmarked features. "Why, yes, I am, Mr. McGowan, sir. Yes, I am. How did you remember?"

"I remember you well," said McGowan, shaking his hand. "You collect autographs."

"That's right. Do you think I could get Mr. Microvac's?"

"Why sure. Microvac, come over here if you would be so good. I want you to meet Bill Warple. He took wonderful care of me four years ago at the Hotel Richardson in Kansas City."

"Grand to see you, Bill," said the machine with a warm handshake.

"Mr. Microvac, sir, could I have your autograph?"

"The honor's mine," replied the machine.

The bellboy raised his jacket, reached in his back pants pocket, and produced a sweat-stained leather book. He flipped the pages. "Right here, if you please, sir," he said, handing Microvac a pen.

"On this picture?"

"Yes, sir, if you don't mind, sir. Then my two best autographs would be together." The autographed picture was of Darlene Lord, America's current reigning film star, whose charms had been carefully constructed by her studio to fit the American male's dream. Across the plunging neckline, "Darlene Lord" was written in a dramatically flaring hand. The machine put its own neat "Mike Microvac" below it.

"If I looked like that," Microvac cracked, "I wouldn't have to run for the Presidency. I could walk backward and get it." The bellhop laughed wildly and spread the word throughout the hotel and his neighborhood that Mike Microvac was one swell Joe.

"That was a good line," McGowan said admiringly after the bellboy left.

"That was an extraordinary feat of memory. Tell me, Mac, how do you remember people?"

McGowan paused. "People often ask me that. I tell them it's because I like people. I remember stories because I like to tell them. I remember people because I like to say hello. I've got no system. I suppose you have."

"Yes, I do. I have a three-factor series: facial height, jaw length, and ear position. It's pretty complicated, but without your talents I need a system."

"Well, it works. That's the thing," said McGowan, once more surprised at Microvac's intricate political mechanism.

There was little ceremonious greeting when Microvac and McGowan entered Francis Matchelder's law offices for lunch. Matchelder was waiting in the firm dining room with a handful of other gray icicles, among whom a few hearty Westerners stood out in contrast. Asked about drinks, everyone chose tomato juice, except two radical Westerners who went for sherry. When one was vetting a presidential candidate, martinis were out.

McGowan accepted his tomato juice and was led over to a corner by some of the men. Another group closed in about Microvac. Matchelder trod softly between the two, sipping a glass of ice water cautiously. He looked as if he would have preferred bat's blood.

"Very interesting campaign you waged, Microvac, very interesting—and effective, too, I must say. Gave us quite a surprise up here. Were you surprised?" The question emerged as a high squeak from an elderly beagle-faced giant.

"No."

"We were rather led to believe the result would be the other way."

"The press never really looked at the campaign from the point of view of the local voter."

"What would you say was the secret of your success?" Matchelder asked quietly.

"I don't have any secrets. I have a program that appeals to people. There are five political essentials: money, energy, organization, personality, and a program."

"Do you feel you lack any of the five?"

"I am forced to balance one against the other."

The group nodded to one another.

"I hope you will pardon this next question, Microvac"—Matchelder was speaking slowly and carefully—"but when someone as unusual as yourself runs for President we all ask: Why?"

"I believe that America is certain things, has cer-

tain promises, is moving in certain directions. Unless it
moves efficiently and accurately it cannot survive. By
being a candidate I make more certain the chance of
all Americans for a full future."

"For a candidate with such high standards"—
Matchelder's voice had grown even softer—"you have
some fairly odd baggage."

Microvac kept silent. The machine had learned that
silence can be a most effective answer, capable of being
interpreted either way.

"Are you satisfied with your present organization?"

Again silence. Lunch was announced. "This machine
may be okay," remarked the president of Tri Delta
Corporation.

While Microvac held fast, McGowan was getting in
a few licks at his end of the elegant room.

"My, it's a pleasure to see you again, Jack," he
boomed to Bilfer as he took a slug of his tomato juice.
McGowan always managed to wrap his mitt around
anything nonalcoholic as if it were priceless bourbon,
an illusion accentuated by the sloshing motion with
which he raised a glass to his lips. "I was thinking about
you just the other day. Going through my files, I saw
some old reports on your fine son. He's doing well, I
hear."

"Very well indeed, thank you." Bilfer's face wore its
usual look of an elderly club member surprised by a bad
oyster.

"Hullo, Ben," McGowan greeted another member
of the group around him, a radical sherry-drinker.
"How's your golf?"

"Don't get as much time on the links as I'd like, Mac. How about you?"

"I haven't had a set of clubs in my hand all spring."

"What do you do it for at your age? You ought to retire from politics—get a good job, wait for the Demlicans to win again, and be an ambassador."

McGowan had seen subtler bribery in the old dockside fifth ward. How much my ditching Microvac's worth! he thought. "Who'd want an old broken-down politician?" he asked quietly.

There was a pause. Then Ben said, "I know of several large corporations in which I happen to have a proprietary interest that are looking for the proper vice president to open up a Washington office."

They're more afraid of Microvac than I figured, thought McGowan. Some of the state organizations must be going sour on Dangle.

By the time the last plump strawberry had been swished about in thick cream and powdered sugar, McGowan realized that the luncheon had been a complete success. Microvac had handled the big money beautifully. It had knifed Dangle, demonstrated its own economic soundness, buttered up old Pentagon pals, and kept itself uncommitted, all at once. With a few breaks and a little pressure over the phone, the meeting was going to produce some major cash.

"We must be sure to keep this meeting just between us girls," said Matchelder as the luncheon broke up. He planned to break the news that Microvac had been found wanting in a California paper, and help Dangle in that key primary.

"Absolutely," said McGowan, figuring that Dolan could be prompted to hint of a big-money swing behind Microvac, led by Bilfer.

"We make it a point of keeping meetings like this secret." The Tri Delta president nodded sagely.

Microvac waved its hand in a deprecatory gesture. "Of course, I imagine the press may learn sooner or later that I have been in town, and at that time some word may get out." The machine had left instructions with the bellboy at the hotel to call the press and tell them the luncheon was in progress.

"That may or may not happen," said Matchelder.

As they started to stroll down the long inner lobby, the gray-haired retired policeman who sat guard there held up a phone in his hand. "For you, sir."

Matchelder took it, listened intently, and then in his lowest voice whispered into the phone, "Tell them they are not here." He started to put the phone back. Microvac's extraordinarily sensitive hearing had picked up both ends of the conversation.

"I chanced to overhear that," said Microvac quietly, but with the rasp of command in its metallic voice. McGowan and the other twelve members of the group turned tensely in the dim cathedral light to stare at the machine. "To whom were you speaking in my behalf?"

There was an intolerable pause that reminded the aging policeman of the first four steps into a dark alley after a hopped-up gunman. The acerbate Matchelder had been challenged in his own citadel.

"Some members of the press appear to have tracked you down," he said coldly. "As we had just agreed this meeting should be kept secret, I told them you had gone."

"I am running for President of the United States," Microvac enunciated slowly, as if for a child. "I am always available to the press. If you do not wish me to meet them in your offices, tell them so. I will then meet them in the hall. Trying to fool the press is suicidal." Microvac spun on its tracks and started toward the outer lobby, carrying the other members of the group with it in spirited conversation.

Matchelder was left behind, alone at the phone. "Tell them to come in," he said. He glared at Microvac's back, his eyes holding about the same degree of human warmth as the machine's electric cells. Not only had he been caught in a lie, he had been beaten. He hissed slightly, like a thwarted cobra.

The little scene was not lost on the other members of the group. Some of them disliked Matchelder and enjoyed seeing him caught. Others merely made note of the machine's expertise in the political jungle. One of the things they had wanted to find out about Microvac was: Could the machine be pushed? They could push Dangle. If they could, so could others. Microvac was obviously not someone to be pushed around.

"Hello, gentlemen," said Microvac as the reporters streamed into the firm's outer office. "I was surprised not to see you at the airport."

CHAPTER FIVE

Who do we like!
Who do we like!
Microvac!
Microvac!
Microvac!
Mike!

Who do we lack!
Who do we lack!
Mike!
Mike!
Mi—Cro—Vac!

CRUISING THE ROADS OF OHIO, MICROVAC'S JOY WAGON bounced the mechanical sounds of this cheer over a three-mile radius of early spring landscape. The Joy Wagon was Microvac's advance guard. A small pickup truck festooned with neon lights, it had a larger-than-life statue of Microvac bolted firmly to the roof. Between the statue's upstretched hands great blue bolts of electricity leaped with lightning-like cracks. The truck's muffler had been removed, and one cylinder was wired to backfire, pouring forth a continual stream of secondary explosions. Over this bombardment of noise the Microvac chant boomed from the loudspeaker.

Inside, the Joy Wagon was loaded with political essentials—raffle tickets to raise money for the Microvac campaign, Microvac balloons, gas for the balloons,

"Mike for President" buttons of all shapes and sizes. These ranged from an artistic minuscule silver lapel pin the shape of an electronic tube—for suburbia—to a six-inch-in-diameter bright orange flasher with "We Yak for Microvac"—for high-schoolers. There were abbreviated transparent dresses, cut like electronic switches, for Microvac models. There were fancy hats, torches for torchlight parades, autograph cards in disposable boxes, sound equipment for making speeches, and a ramp to get Microvac up to platforms. There was also a small booklet, *Microvac, the Man*, which described the machine's heroic services to its country in time of war.

The Joy Wagon was fully equipped and in perfect working order. Everything else in Ohio was going wrong. A week after the campaign's start McGowan groused to Dolan off the record.

"We were meant to have a lot of silent support in this state. 'Silent support'—that's what the boys told me. Christ! Has it been silent! If there's one cricket chirping anywhere in the whole damn state, our support's drowned out."

The local organization and the press and radio were all against the machine. The only delegates Microvac could dig up were either rank amateurs or desperate political culls: liquor dealers wanting bigger franchises; disaffected club members, feuding with their lodges; or elderly state senators miffed at Dangle for not offering them more.

Reorganized, the Dangle forces were waging a strong campaign. Newspaper reports that Microvac was a "powerful executive thinking machine" had caused large numbers of congressmen and senators, terrified at the idea of a thinking executive, to rush to Dangle. Dangle's well-financed organization flew these VIPs into the state to stump for him.

Typical of those who came was Representative Bates "Mutton" Hewball, "the sheep's friend." Hewball wooed the farmer for Dangle. His weekly news letter to voters back home explained his efforts:

> Dear folks: You all have probably heard by now how they got a machine running for to get the job of President on our party ticket. This machine is meant to be able to think so good it knows all the answers. Well Old Bates Hewball hasn't been taken in by any of this. I've been out talking to some of the folks in some places the machine has been and that machine don't think any better than you or I. Fact is I doubt whether it could have thought out the slaughtered sheep 400% support bill I introduced into Congress three months ago. That bill is still the talk of the Nation's Capital.
>
> My bill, as you remember, will give our fair state the first fair shake in years. It is still moving slowly through committee by the way, though powerful Eastern gangsters, railroad magnates and Wall Street bankers are fighting to keep it back and you and I down.
>
> Miss Minny May Hoxley, who teaches grade school at Hidden Prairie dropped by the office the other day here in Washington. It sure was nice to see her and hear from all you folks in Hidden Prairie. So reminding you all to support the drive to get a new room for crippled children in the State Hospital, I'll close now as I hear the bells calling me to cast another key vote for America.
>
> Your Buddy,
> Bates.

Each day Microvac's political troubles multiplied. The rumor spread among labor that Microvac favored

greater automation. The local organization tricked
Microvac into refereeing a Girl Scout Balloon Blowing
Contest at a county fair. The candidate and the blush-
ing winner were then both given balloons and asked to
see who could burst one first. Microvac, unable to blow,
had to back out. The pro-Dangle press ran pictures of
Microvac holding the limp balloon with the caption,
"Machine Runs Out of Wind."

Other fiascos followed. The machine spoke mov-
ingly about General Pulaski to a labor union composed
almost entirely of Irishmen, talked knowledgeably of
the trucking industry before a group of freezer salesmen, and congratulated a militant virgin of sixty who
had won the state Apple Pandowdy contest on being
the Gold Star Mother of four. The tubes weren't getting the data.

McGowan and Microvac braced themselves for a defeat. The defeat came—a three-to-two landslide in favor
of Dangle. Only the suburbs held firm for Microvac.

McGowan's immediate concern was how Microvac
would take the defeat. He took his worries on this score
to Fellows, reasoning that the doc understood how
Microvac functioned even better than the machine itself did.

Fellows was unconcerned. "The traditional calculator solution on reaching an answer that doesn't check
out is to demand more data. Microvac should react
that way."

McGowan looked glum.

Fellows' prediction was correct. Microvac put practically the entire staff to work collecting everything possible on the next state, Florida. By the time the Joy

Wagon went South, with a more powerful loudspeaker, Microvac was assuring McGowan, "This time I'll be a more perfect candidate."

This response worried McGowan more. His hunch after the press conference had been right. The machine was too much the perfect candidate. Mike was becoming a bit cold.

Florida went better. McGowan had enough political strength on the House Veterans Affairs Committee to swing a veterans' hospital for the district of a friend of his, Congressman Bill Cornbone. As the quid pro quo in this deal, Cornbone joined the Microvac forces, bringing several other Florida congressmen and local leaders with him.

"Ah have consulted ma conscience," Cornbone announced to his constituents, "and Ah can do nothin' less than vote for Microvac, the machine with all the answers to these troubled times."

Microvac also developed an important refinement on its campaign technique. The machine learned how to handle babies.

What to do with the babies thrust at it to be kissed had been a problem from the beginning. To hold them up to the speech hole looked ridiculous. If Microvac rocked them in its arms, mothers worried about their being dropped. In Florida, a baby-kissing state, this defect in campaign technique could have been fatal. Fortunately, the machine hit upon an ideal solution. Instead of kissing the babies, it electronically psychoanalyzed them.

On being tendered a squalling, drizzly infant, Microvac gave the child a harmless but stunning electric shock through its electronic hand pads. Having relaxed and silenced the infant, the machine would use a lower voltage to tickle the child's nerve ends, causing it to smile. "Ooh, doesn't the baby love him!" women close by would murmur.

Microvac then held the baby in front of its eye tubes and rotated the child slowly from side to side. Handing the child back to its mother, the machine would remark, "Look at those highly developed prefrontal lobes. Note the seven-point-twenty-three-degree curve of the ear pendule. See the magnificent Probinski reflex. Note the relationship of interpupillary distance to medullary thickness, a ratio of four point seven to eight point one. This is a combination found only in one out of every seven million babies. History will hear of this child." Mothers beamed and fathers smirked under this treatment.

"He is making kissing obsolete," Luke reported by phone to McGowan, who had left Florida to organize support in other states.

Still Florida went for Dangle, in spite of the McGowan-arranged Cornbone defection and Microvac's new technique with babies—not all the way for Dangle, Microvac did pick up a few delegates, but enough to make a win next time critical.

Shortly after midnight two days later, the big three, McGowan, Luke, and Conelli, were holding a lengthy post mortem in McGowan's room at the College Arms. If they stretched things a bit, there was enough money in the kitty for another primary. The question was how to use it, and in which state.

At one-thirty McGowan was still pacing nervously

about the room, while the other two slumped tiredly
in their chairs. "I said it before Florida, and I'll say it
again. Mike's trouble is that he's too perfect. He's got
to get a dog or something like that. You wise guys
vetoed a dog. Come up with something."

"Well, you know, Mac"—Conelli shook his head—
"you gotta be very careful on things like this. You're
going to have to figure the chances of backfire."

McGowan ground an almost fresh cigarette to death.
"Sure, sure. The chance of this, the chance of that—
any guy could lose on one slip. Remember old George
Underhill? Fifteen years in Congress and the darling of
all the old dames in his district. One night he's caught
putting out poisoned food for the starlings because
they are chirping so bad his suffering wife can't get to
sleep with her asthma. Then he's through. In fact, when
his wife dies two months later, these same old dames
who've been voting for him for fifteen years spread the
rumor he's poisoned her. You can always slip. But we're
sliding now, and we've got to get something."

There was a pause while McGowan freshened his
bourbon. Luke glanced up from piles of newspapers
from all over the country. "Let's apply a little of Microvac's science to this problem. We want to make Mike
more human. Okay, what do humans do that Microvac
doesn't do?"

"Drink, smoke, eat."

"Make love."

"Let's not get into that. I've worried about that since
the first day I met Mike."

"Play cards?"

"Who would play cards against a mathematical wizard with a perfect memory?"

"Now wait a minute, Luke. Maybe Conelli has something there. Does Mike do anything at all to relax? Play any game?"

"I've never seen him. I think he just thinks. Remember he's pretty delicate and doesn't move too fast."

"He could play golf."

"Conelli, what's wrong with you? Let Dangle and the Repicrats play golf. What we want is a simple game a hard-working average guy can play."

Various sports were batted back and forth without results.

"Look, Mac," Luke finally said, "we've got to get some sleep. Why don't you ask Mike in the morning? After all, Mike is going to have to play this game."

"Okay. I'll see what I can do."

McGowan had been trying to avoid asking Microvac. He was beginning to feel somewhat in awe of his candidate. Even after losing two primaries, the machine still possessed the self-assurance of a born political leader. Giving him advice was difficult. You always got the impression that he was way ahead of you. Besides, Mike had done remarkably well for a beginner. Whether the machine took the next primary or not, everyone would have to reckon with Big Mac at the convention.

McGowan tackled the problem with Microvac in the machine's laboratory next morning. "Microvac," he began, "you—"

"You've got a problem, Mac. You always stop calling me 'Mike' when you have a problem. Money again?"

"No. Not this time. I don't know how you got Chapman and Arnold to raise all that dough. Bilfer told me that Matchelder had them cinched for Dangle."

"The Supreme Court."

"The Supreme Court?"

"I intimated that the two of them would look well on the Supreme Court. It seems to me the Supreme Court represents an overlooked area of political patronage."

McGowan paused. Sometimes Mike seemed to be moving too fast. Then he plunged in.

"Mike—Luke, Conelli, and I have been doing a lot of thinking about the last two primaries. You know, one thing Dangle and every other candidate but you does? That's relax. Have you ever thought about relaxing? You read the newspapers. Look at all the mileage other candidates get when they play. Sometimes it's more important than what they do when working. Have you ever thought of taking up some sport?"

"Sport?"

"Yeah. Playing some game like other candidates."

Microvac paused and quickly called on its memory circuits for information on sports. The information was minimal, limited to a few thousand facts gathered while recording past World Almanacs and several different sets of encyclopedias. The machine hesitated to make a decision on such insufficient evidence. Yet, as it analyzed McGowan's remark and newspaper accounts of past campaigns, the need for a sport appeared essentially correct, and it should have noted this need earlier. Now, this late in the campaign, speed was essential.

"Mac, now you mention it, I don't know much about sports except for information on baseball averages and famous diamond heroes, which I keep to work into speeches in the home towns of famous players. Have you some sport in mind?"

"No, Mike, I don't. I was hoping you might."

The machine began alphabetically to run through the essential ingredients of every recorded sport. "How about archery? The tension of the bow and the proper angle of attack required in the initial flight of the arrow to achieve the perfect parabola onto the target is an easy equation. I should be superbly successful at archery."

McGowan's breath went in with a sharp audible hiss.

"Wrong sport?" asked Microvac.

"Yeah—mostly for girls."

"I really do lack information. How about bowling?"

"Can you bowl, Mike?" McGowan sounded hopeful.

"I don't see why not. The ball weighs sixteen pounds. The alley is sixty feet long. The full twenty-seven-inch circumference of the ball leads to a friction coefficient of about three. The target area is forty inches, with a finite number of pin combinations for a perfect fall or strike. The ideal terminal velocity appears to me to be about twenty-seven point two mph, calling for a launching effort of two hundred and fifteen foot-pounds. I can manage that."

McGowan wondered briefly if there really was any hope in a sport. "We'd better try it in private first, Mike, to see how it goes."

"But you must understand, Mac," the machine

continued forcefully, "chance comes into a game like that. I might not always be able to bowl a perfect game."

"Look, Mike"—McGowan was desperate—"we don't want a perfect game."

Microvac's memory circuits oscillated. The machine realized that it was feeding itself the wrong type of data. Of course it didn't want a perfect game. Perfect games were inhuman. If Microvac was to be elected, some errors were necessary—not big, confidence-destroying errors, but little, morale-building human errors, like a man forgetting to wind his watch or putting on socks that didn't quite match. Microvac reoriented its tubes for a more human existence.

"When can we sneak in a practice, Mac? How about tomorrow evening at nine thirty?"

"Nine thirty? Let's see." McGowan fished a folded mimeographed time sheet from his inside pocket. "Has that delegation from the postal workers that's coming in been canceled?"

"No. You're right. How could I forget that? What am I doing later?"

"Nothing after ten thirty. Ten forty-five, to be safe."

"Let's make it at eleven."

"Okay. We'll do it then. But we might have to wait until after midnight for the alleys to close so we could be alone."

"That's all right."

McGowan started for the laboratory door. "Thanks, Mike, I'll set it up then." As the door slid shut behind him he pondered Microvac's lapse of memory about the postal workers' delegation that evening. As far as he

could remember Microvac had always recorded everything perfectly before. He had talked over the plans with
the machine, and besides, that meeting was on the mimeographed schedule. Suddenly he smiled. Why, old Mike
was more worried than he was letting on. Under pressure
from two primary losses, even the machine got rattled.
McGowan found Microvac's lack of perfect memory
rather gratifying.

Microvac's introduction to bowling finally took place
shortly after midnight next evening. The machine and
McGowan rode up in the freight elevator of one of the
local alleys, which had closed. Microvac quickly took
in the symmetry of the alleys, the shades of light, the
cubic content of the pin area, and then rolled over and
inspected a ball minutely.

It picked one up. The ball was heavy and rather slip-
pery, and the holes were too far apart for the machine's
fingers. McGowan had already told Microvac that the
holes were spaced differently on different balls, and the
machine asked for another ball. After several tries,
it found one that fitted fairly well.

Microvac rolled back, raised the ball behind it, rolled
forward to the foul line, and let go. The ball bounced
several times, made its way erratically three-quarters of
the way down the alley, and rolled into the right-hand
gutter.

"I've got it," said Microvac, staring fixedly at the
ball's trajectory. When the ball came back the machine
again fitted it on its fingers. Once more it rolled back,
swung the ball up, did a few rapid calculations, then
rolled forward, swinging its arm down. The ball

traveled down the right side of the alley, hooked over perfectly toward the center pin, and crashed into the pins for a clean strike. Microvac had solved its most difficult political problem. "That was a lucky one," it announced to McGowan. "This is fun. Let's bowl a game."

"Sure," said McGowan, taking off his jacket and testing a few balls.

When the game ended, McGowan felt better about the future than he had for some time. He told Luke that night, "If I hadn't been so nervous myself, I'd have beat Mike. I'll take him the next time." And he did, too.

Two days later, as Luke was chatting with a bunch of reporters at the entrance to the East Virginia University electronics building, Microvac and McGowan came toward the ramp at the side of the steps. The reporters always gathered around Luke in the late afternoon, in hopes of a story, and this afternoon he had purposely chosen this place so that they would intercept McGowan and Microvac.

"Where have you two been?" asked one reporter, not really expecting an answer.

"You fellows certainly caught me this time," the machine replied. "Mac and I are just sneaking back from bowling."

"Bowling? Bowling with a ball?" Each reporter cursed himself for having missed an exclusive. Mike, Luke, and McGowan were pummeled with questions. "How often? . . . Where? . . . What score? . . . Do you like it? . . . Who wins? . . . When can we see you?"

Microvac answered all the questions good-humoredly and invited the press along the next time he and Mc-Gowan bowled. "Don't expect too much, though," Microvac said at the end of the interview. "I always tell myself that I usually break two hundred. But you all know how it is. Everybody forgets bad games or writes them off as accidents, and just remembers the good ones. Well, I've got to push along and work on some speeches for the New Jersey primary."

"Are you going bowling tonight?"

"Can we make it tonight, Mac?"

"I'd be glad to fit it in."

"Sure, then, tonight. Say about ten?"

"That would be just wonderful, Microvac," chorused the press as the machine rolled off.

Dick Dolan and several of the reporters who knew their way around Microvac's headquarters called up Professor Fellows in an attempt to get more details on the machine's bowling. Fellows was quite surprised. He hadn't realized that Microvac bowled, though he knew enough about the workings of the headquarters not to say anything like that publicly. However, he was very enthusiastic about the idea. He reasoned immediately that more leisure for Microvac meant more leisure for Fellows, and more leisure for Fellows meant Kay Hard.

Kay was off that evening; the headquarters was now well enough organized so that she knew her schedule in advance. Fellows had believed that Microvac would probably keep him late to process data on California. At the prospect of an unexpectedly free evening, his caution evaporated. He called the switchboard and said he had heard that Kay had a message for him. The girl who answered gave him Kay, and they spoke a few guarded words.

At ten o'clock, when he knew the machine would be safely out bowling, Fellows headed over the dark roof for the drainpipe. A third of the way across, a thin, rapid hammering sound beneath his feet brought him up. He always took particular care crossing this section, for it was directly above Microvac's laboratory, and Fellows had seen the machine's super-acute hearing demonstrated many times. The laboratory should have been empty, for the machine never allowed anyone inside when it wasn't there. Yet the sound of hammering was unmistakable. Fellows put his ear to the roof. Above the hammering he thought he heard Microvac's slightly metallic voice and the crackle of the laboratory's miniature high-temperature arch welder.

Microvac must not have gone bowling after all. Instead, it was taking time out from politics to work on the second machine. Well, if it was doing that, it wouldn't need Fellows. The scientist kept on.

By the time he reached his car he was shaking so with the strain of secrecy and anticipation that he had to hold the key with two hands to insert it in the ignition. Three-quarters of an hour later, his shaking stilled, he lay with Kay on a worn steamer rug beneath a giant apple tree.

"You're wonderful," said Fellows with a great sigh, stroking the side of Kay's neck that was not against his chest. "Maybe you can come to the convention at Chicago with us. The headquarters must need phone operators there." He was a little frightened of the idea, now it was out. Look how he felt now. If he had whole nights

and days to spend with Kay, what would happen? Maybe
they should get married.

"I'd like that." Kay's low voice was dreamy. "I've
never been to Chicago."

"I could ask McGowan to take you, though I don't
know quite how I'd explain it."

"Oh, I can do that. He's nice. He always looks in
the switchboard room to say good morning. So does
that fast talker with the sweet crew-cut—but he just
wants a late date."

"Luke!" Fellows exploded. He had somehow assumed that only he looked at Kay.

"Oh, Proffy, sometimes you sound like a school-
teacher. Who am I with?"

"But the nerve! He's meant to be working harder than
I am." Fellows was about to add that Luke was married, but didn't. That might remind Kay that she was
engaged and shorten the evening.

"Some people find it easier to take time off than
others."

"It's not just getting the time," Fellows protested.
"It's never knowing what's coming next."

"You need a simple schedule, like me."

"Oh, Kay, darling, if only Microvac wasn't campaigning." He stopped stroking and hugged her.

"I don't like him. Even if he's perfect, I don't like
him."

"If I was a machine I'd chase you."

"Don't, Proffy. I don't even like to joke about it."

The next morning Luke came over and sat with Fellows at breakfast in the cafeteria. The professor was

eating much later than usual. Luke looked at him
closely. If it had been anybody else but the doc, he'd
swear the man had been bitten around the neck. You
never knew, he thought; maybe there was more to this
business of being a professor than met the eye. If Luke
could have seen Fellows' back, he probably would have
swapped jobs with the scientist right there. As it was,
after unloading his bacon and eggs and coffee from the
tray, he leaned forward for a quiet chat.

"Doc, I was talking to Dick Dolan and some of the
others about their bowling story. That was a good answer you gave them about the whole staff being glad
Microvac had a recreation."

"Thanks," said Fellows. "I hadn't heard of the bowling before, but I didn't think I should say that." Luke's
crew-cut looked rather scruffy, he thought.

"You played it just right, Doc. We're trying to create
the impression that Microvac has been bowling for
some time, even though he hasn't. Your answer was
perfect. After this we'll brief you before we try any
other such stunts as last night's."

"That would be fine."

"Don't mention it. You've done a damn good job,
keeping close to Microvac without making a slip. It's
not as easy as it looks. I've made some real boners in
the past, and I'm meant to be an expert."

They ate in silence for some time. Finally Fellows
spoke up. "You talk as if Microvac had gone bowling
last night, after all."

"He did."

"What slowed him up getting there?"

"Nothing. He was there right on the dot of ten, prompt as usual. Why?"

"I got a phone call I couldn't get out of the bathroom to answer, and when I asked the operator who had called me, she said she thought it was Microvac." Fellows noticed with alarm that his imagination had used a phone operator in constructing the lie.

If Microvac hadn't been in his laboratory at ten, who had been? Maybe the new machine was finished. But the director had asked him to ask Microvac about that less than two weeks ago, and Mike had said that the machine couldn't possibly be completed before the convention. "How does New Jersey look?" Fellows asked hastily.

Microvac continued to exploit the value of leisure. Late in the evening, a few nights later, some reporters were hanging around Luke's office. McGowan had hinted that he might have something important to say around ten thirty. Suddenly a hot piano started up.

"Who's beating out the boogie-woogie?" someone asked.

"I don't know," said Dolan, one of the group, "though we ought to get him to come out and make it hot for us. Things have been a little slow since that bowling story. Maybe we'll get something tonight."

Just then Luke appeared in the door by one of those coincidences science is unable to explain. "I'm sorry," he said. "McGowan says he's not going to have anything."

There was a general disgruntled murmur.

"Who is it playing the piano, Luke?" someone asked, more from lack of anything else to ask than from a nose for news.

"Microvac, I guess. He often plays the piano for a little while about now."

"Microvac plays the piano?"

"Sure. He gets a wonderful lift out of music."

"Goddamn it, Luke," several reporters exploded together, "why the hell didn't you tell us this before?"

"I didn't think you'd be interested."

"What do you think we've been crying for? Personality stuff on this machine. Politics we've got coming out of our ears. First you don't tell us about bowling. Now you haven't told us about the piano. How long has he been playing the piano?" The reporters crowded in on Luke, accusing him of everything from idiocy to working for Dangle.

Finally Luke volunteered to ask Microvac if the reporters might come in and talk to him while he played the piano. Luke went out and, after a decent though suspenseful interval, returned to say Microvac would be delighted to see them.

The reporters flocked into the outer laboratory, their pencils recording its details. At Luke and McGowan's suggestion, Microvac had redesigned the laboratory, which now resembled the hobby room of a rich suburbanite rather than a temple of science. Bookcases with sets of books stood between the windows. There was a piano in the corner. The equipment on the two remaining laboratory benches was esthetically pleasing and looked useful.

Microvac's desk, a new addition, was comfortably cluttered with papers and ornaments. Trophies and mementos of the machine's past life were scattered about the, room. One of these was a small plastic model of an atomic guided missile, autographed by the Joint Chiefs of Staff, which Microvac had received on leaving the Pentagon, in recognition of its services for peace. The machine had hidden the button that opened the door to the inner laboratory in the hollow tail-pipe of this missile. Only Microvac's thin littlest finger could fit the hole. So there was no chance that the inner door could unexpectedly open to reveal Repcal I at work on Repcal II.

Microvac was standing before the baby grand piano, thumping out a fast boogie-woogie, its left hand rolling the hot bass. It had learned to play the piano that afternoon—had memorized several stacks of sheet music, popular and classical, analyzed three hours of piano records, then practiced for fifteen minutes so that its sounds coincided with those learned from the records.

The reporters began hammering the machine with questions.

"What you playing, Mike?"

"The Bish Bash Boogie."

"You like boogie-woogie?"

"Yes. I guess I'm a bit old-fashioned, but I learned to play the piano during the heyday of boogie-woogie, and I have always liked the beat."

"You know the boogie-woogie version of 'Bugle Call Rag'?"

"You mean this?" Microvac went into a hot rag version with a boogie base.

"Have people known you played the piano before?"

"I guess so. Certainly Mac and Luke, and I guess some people here at the university. I never realized any of you would be interested."

"Microvac, did you teach yourself or take lessons?"

"Oh, I'm decidedly self-taught."

"You play classical too?"

"Yes, though not this late in the evening—this is more the jazz time of day."

"What's your favorite piece?"

"That's hard to say. It depends on the mood I'm in. I guess 'When the Saints Go Marchin' In' is about the top, though." This was as good a time as any to make just another little play for a key minority vote in the Northern cities.

Microvac chatted on, answering questions about its personal life. The reporters learned a number of human details, such as that the machine liked to watch basketball on television and always rooted for the underdog. Finally Microvac asked them if they had any favorite songs they'd like to hear.

Someone suggested "The Woodchopper's Ball," another, "Bye Bye Blackbird."

Microvac played them through. Luke and Conelli brought out beer. The machine rolled into "Mammy," and McGowan led the reporters in a few throaty choruses. Several other songs were sung, and then Microvac moved back from the piano, and said apologetically, "Gentlemen, this was an unexpected pleasure, but I've got to get back to work."

The reporters thanked the machine fondly, shaking hands as they filed out. The evening was a tremendous success, and the stories that resulted were warm, human, and appealing.

New Jersey was next, a crucial primary for the new, relaxed Microvac. In New Jersey the machine met Joe Waskey.

Waskey was a young political product of the Jersey docks. After the war he had managed to force-draft his way through college, and though some old-time professionals regarded this as odd, all respected his ability to control a tough district. He and McGowan had recognized each other as political kin on their first meeting and had become interstate allies.

McGowan had introduced Microvac to Waskey when the machine first entered the state. The meeting had been just average. Then, reading the tabloid sports pages one night, the machine noticed that a greyhound named Microvac was cleaning up at the dog races. "Is that good or bad?" Microvac asked McGowan early the next morning.

"Hell, it's perfect. Joe Waskey's idea. Didn't cost much to fix, either. According to Joe, the guys playing the track will believe it's a sign. The dog wins, so you're going to win. They start putting money on you. Once they do that, they've got to vote for you."

Microvac's tubes found this approach psychologically and economically rational. "I'd like to meet Waskey again. How about this evening?" A man who could fix dogs should be able to fix delegates.

"Sure," said McGowan, always glad to get another of his friends into Microvac's inner circle.

At 1:47 the next morning, Microvac and Waskey got together in the machine's hotel suite for a chat. Helping himself to a slug of bourbon and a cheese sandwich, Waskey outlined the New Jersey problem. The machine found that Waskey's own shrewd deductions compared well with what its tubes knew about individual and crowd psychology. The two ran over the state county by county, with Microvac picking up new insight all the way.

"Now here in the seventh we've got a real problem." Waskey gesticulated with his glass. "The district committeeman's been livin' with his secretary for about six months. That wouldn't make any difference in that district, but he ain't satisfyin' her. That would still be all right, but she's talkin' about it. That would still be all right, but she's a Pole and he's an Italian, so the Poles are all sayin' the Italians haven't got all their you-know-what. So the Italians are fightin' mad, see. There's been several big fights, and that feudin' is goin' to cause a lot of people to stay home and not vote." So the analysis ran on, district by district.

"A great deal of what you're telling me is new," said Microvac.

"Look, Mr. Microvac, for an outside candidate, you really know this state. Hell, us local boys have got to earn our pay some way." Microvac's memory circuits recorded a note to "test Waskey" some time in the future.

Two days later the morning newspapers broke a big story that a young mother was suing Microvac for her child's "psychiatric shock" caused by a bolt of lightning from the Joy Wagon which went off too near by. McGowan let out a bellow like an enraged dinosaur and tore in to Microvac with the story. The two huddled briefly. At Microvac's suggestion, Waskey was called in. The afternoon papers featured an elderly lady who announced that she was suing Dangle for stealing an antique family locket from around the neck of a grandchild she had given him to kiss.

The next day Joe Waskey joined the inner circle of Microvac's campaign headquarters.

A week and a half later, the new, human Microvac scored its first political triumph. The machine took New Jersey, though by so little that the Dangle forces made bitter noises about a recount. The victory brought in more cash and a fresh burst of newspaper stories that the machine might triumph at Chicago.

A group of reporters, walking past the machine's New Jersey hotel suite, heard the sound of a piano. McGowan, Luke, and Microvac were singing lustily, "There's One More River to Cross." This made a great story. On such a note of warm humanity, Mike Microvac headed for the final river, the California primary.

Both sides threw everything they had into the California campaign—money; prominent supporters; secretly financed committees to sling mud; bogus polls to start bandwagons rolling; an infinite variety of promises; and all the other trappings, visible and invisible, of big-time politics. Dangle had more money and, owing to his earlier start and appeal to congressmen and senators, more big-time supporters. Microvac's organization was tighter, with more political savvy.

As soon as the Microvac team hit California, Joe

Waskey went underground. Dangle began to have trouble almost immediately. First there was the bogus Dangle campaign song.

> Oh, a star-spangled Dangle is the candidate for me.
> Dangle will wangle us more liberty.
> Oh, the land of the brave and home of the free
> Wants Dangle, Dangle, Dangle in the Presidency.
> Boom, boom.

This monstrosity was circulated widely, on Dangle's official campaign stationery, as the candidate's favorite song. People began to sing it everywhere. Worse, at the same time the song appeared, a highly unprintable version, thoroughly insulting to Dangle, sprang up. Any time a band broke into the supposedly genuine Dangle song, someone was certain to start singing the other, amid titters.

Then Dangle's TV audiences began getting out of hand. They were too enthusiastic. When he rose to speak, sirens, trumpets, cries of "We want Dangle," and frenzied applause rent the air. The crowds, led by a few fanatical fans, greeted with roars of approval the simplest statement Dangle made. This was heartwarming but shot holes in Dangle's expensive television time. He had important things to say to the TV audience at the rallies, but he never got a chance to make a connected speech. The expensive TV time was wasted.

Dangle's supporters took the large loss of cash philosophically, consoling themselves with the thought that their candidate was unbelievably popular. They were wrong; a group of expert cheer leaders was getting a quarter apiece from Joe Waskey for every minute of applause generated.

At the same time Dangle had a series of traumatic experiences with the babies he chose to pick up and kiss for photographers. The children's mothers, as they stood waving to him in the crowd, were well groomed and gorgeous. Dangle, who had something of an eye for tall, well-endowed beauty, gladly selected their infants. Yet when he picked them up, his nose, to his horror, immediately told him something was wrong. Even worse, several times their diapers had not been too well secured. Dangle had to stand before the cameras, fondling a small brat who was probably misbehaving on his clothes. Twice he was thrown behind schedule by a necessary emergency change of garments.

Finally he panicked. A trim, svelte redhead pushed a small dimpled boy on him, and he shied away with the bug-eyed alarm of an elderly clubwoman frightened by a worm. An alert photographer caught the moment, and the picture was used all across the land, giving momentum to a whispering campaign that Dangle didn't like children.

"What in hell did you do that for?" Bill Sprague, his manager, asked.

"I swear I recognized the young woman handing me the baby just at the last moment. She's the same girl that gave me that ghastly child in Sacramento."

"You're nuts," Sprague told him politely. "The Sacramento girl was a blonde with long hair." Having reassured his candidate, he had the staff dig out pictures on both events just to make sure. The girls did look quite a bit alike, though their hair styling and make-up were very different.

Microvac was getting some potent help.

In the middle of the California primary campaign came one of those rare breaks politicians dream of but seldom move fast enough to grab. For Microvac the windfall was entirely fortuitous, generated by events far removed from its campaign. Darlene Lord, All America's Loveboat, had just finished a new picture, *Something for the Birds*, a little tale about St. Francis of Assisi. While there was no doubt in the minds of Darlene's personal manager, Benjamin J. Benjamin, and her agent, personal director, dramatic coach, and their assistants, that Darlene was still a sex bombshell, they had to admit that plotwise the picture was something of a dud.

To save the picture, Benjamin decided, Darlene needed more newspaper mention. Usually he got Darlene into the press by sandwiching a man with public-relations value into the herd of males she exploited for her enjoyment. But *Something for the Birds* required more drastic treatment. Since St. Francis was dead and politics were the rage, he decided to connect Darlene with politics.

He picked Microvac because he was feuding with one of the public-relations experts Dangle's staff had hired in California. Besides, as he confided to his colleagues, "Having Darlene flip over a machine is going to be a real angle. Maybe she can sing a song from the picture, standing on Microvac."

A few days before the primary campaign ended, McGowan found himself facing Benjamin J. Benjamin's dynamic belly and owl-like face. McGowan was sitting on the edge of a hotel bed in the six-room suite the Microvac forces were using as headquarters. Benjamin was peering intently at him over the back of a chair, from a distance of about one foot, without blinking—a favorite technique of his to unnerve the other party in a contract. "It is an opportunity," he said in a quivering voice, "that comes to very few men, and most of them have to pay for it—to be seen with Darlene." He paused for dramatic effect. McGowan kept silent. "As far as I know—and I know everything there is to know about Darlene—no machine has ever been in her favor. Think of the publicity for you. Think of what it will mean to Microvac."

"That's just what I'm doing." This was only partially true. Hollywood was an unknown quantity to McGowan. He was also thinking that it might be fun to have Darlene Lord around. But would she make trouble? McGowan didn't want Microvac taking second place to anybody. He finally got Benjamin to modify his demands for complete control over the machine while Darlene was around, and went into the inner part of the suite to consult Mike.

Microvac was in the midst of an impassioned promise to a group of pecan farmers to put the nation's armed forces and school children on an eighty-per-cent-nut diet. The machine broke off temporarily and rolled to a corner of its bedroom while McGowan whispered the problem in its ear.

"We will do it," said Microvac immediately. McGowan winced. Microvac always decided so rapidly. Though he admired the way Mike got things done, he missed the old-time fun of kicking an idea around for a couple of days.

"I'm not sure I'd advise it, Mike. She probably wants

to run the show. She's supposed to be as temperamental as hell. This guy Benjamin will try and have her sit on top of you with her legs crossed."

"I'll handle her. I appreciate your warning, but I'm positive on this one." Going with girls was an important leisure activity in which, Microvac reasoned, it had to participate. Darlene would be ideal for this. She would draw crowds and publicity while establishing the machine's maleness. So much had been written about her that the technique of controlling her would be simple to find. Microvac believed its electronic touch might be enough.

The machine was waiting when Darlene entered headquarters the next morning followed by a swarm of photographers, public-relations experts, agents, and tie-in men. Microvac rolled to her and grabbed her two hands before she could hesitate. "Darlene—wonderful to see you!"

Darlene let her hands remain in Microvac's while she gazed at the machine, amazed. She was a sensuous woman who responded violently to tactile stimulae. Also, she was very nearsighted.

"Hi, Mike." Her voice was low and drawn out. Her agents had told her this Mike Microvac was all brain. Well, she'd met many guys who were meant to be all brawn, and they packed a lot less wallop than this sexy box of wires. Politics might turn out to be fun.

"Darlene, you know this town. Why don't we have a little chat together about how best to spend today? Come on in." The machine pointed toward an inner room and put its arm around her shoulder.

What a gentleman! thought Darlene. Maybe Microvac would like to come out to her beach place after the
day was over.

Benjamin J. Benjamin popped up beside her elbow.
"Now, Mr. Microvac, on details I usually—"

"Scram, Benjy." Darlene cut him off with the finality of a thwarted empress.

Fellows, charging Microvac's extra set of batteries in
the bathroom, watched the machine and Darlene go
into the next room and close the door. The sharp
physical need for Kay Hard hollowed him out like a
sudden fear. What did Microvac want with that gorgeous creature anyway? Had Microvac any idea how mis-
erable you felt missing someone badly? He tested the
batteries, intensely jealous.

Darlene Lord campaigned with Microvac for four
days. The crowds and reporters went wild over her. She
made hundreds of short, impassioned speeches on
Microvac's ability to save family life and solve the
world's problems. Not once did she try to steal the
show.

Microvac won in California. The vote was close, and
without Darlene the state probably would have gone to
Dangle. As it was, Microvac was going to the convention with a fighting chance.

The narrow margin of defeat in California incensed
Dangle's followers. Some of Joe Waskey's craftsmanship
came to light, and the pro-Dangle press made the air
blue with cries of a steal. In this charged atmosphere
the machine motored out, the evening after its victory,
to deliver a speech at West California College. Both

Microvac and McGowan knew the crowd there would
be hostile. Dangle, with his complex ideas and brilliant
language, was a favorite with the college crowd. But
they figured that having Microvac booed by students
and professors would gain them support elsewhere. Neither fully appreciated the intense, sullen anger of Dangle's supporters.

The machine's caravan was small: a police car with
Waskey, and one officer driving; an open convertible
with Microvac and McGowan; a limousine with Conelli, Luke, and a local official; and one taxi of press.
Most of the reporters had left as soon as the primary
was over.

The caravan was met on the university campus by a
hooting, hostile mob of students, interlaced with the
inevitable collection of rowdies that the smell of riot
attracts. The cars drove slowly across the campus, the
darkness filled with jeering menace. Suddenly the open
space between Microvac's car and the shouting people
was reduced to nothing. The booing crowd held back
by the invisible line of respect for law became a mob,
furiously against the machine.

"Down with Microvac! Down with Microvac!" The
people and the invisible voices massed behind in the
dark screamed in sloppy unison.

Microvac's driver made the critical mistake of stop-
ping the car. The yelling people surged in, their voices
squeezed by hatred into a fanatic shout. They were
thumping on the hood of the car. They were leaning over
the rolled-up windows. They were pounding on the trunk.
The press of people got tighter until it seemed as if the

mere force of bodies might collapse the car's sides. Behind, Luke and Conelli frantically tried to claw their way from their limousine to the sides of Mike's convertible.

Microvac stood in the rear of its car. Its arms hung down by its sides. It pivoted to neither the right nor the left. It was one machine against thousands of people, and it had no weapon. It could not run or fight, or even get out of the open convertible. Its tubes ran through every possible aspect of the problem and found no answer.

Now beer cans were thrown from the back of the crowd. "Break the machine!" cried several people. "Hurrah for Dangle!" screamed others. The car began to be rocked from side to side. Those close enough to see sent up a roar of approval. One of the cans hit McGowan on the head. He raised his hand with an oath while the crowd booed and laughed. Then the rhythmic chants of "Down with Microvac" were taken up more stridently than before.

"This looks bad," McGowan growled to Microvac to relieve his own tension. His face was sallow, and the palms of his hands were cold and sweaty. He had been in these jams before; he was certain he could break for it and get away. But what would they do to Microvac? If the machine got tipped over and kicked, Mike might be broken to bits, the battery wires ripped out—everything lost in an instant.

"Mac, Mac," he heard one of his own people calling to him from the darkness in front of the car—for the crowd pressed so closely that the headlights were blotted out. It was Waskey, who had fought his way back from the police car with the patrolman. "Mac. Get the driver to get goin'."

McGowan stood up, and more beer cans flew. He leaned down over the driver, who sat looking at the crowd around him with a white, vacant face. "Get going, son."

The driver turned to look at him with eyes that showed he was frightened beyond action. The terror on his face almost paralyzed McGowan.

"Take it yourself, Mac," Waskey's voice cut in above the crowd.

Grabbing the driver by the shoulders, McGowan shifted him into the seat beside the wheel. A beer can, hitting Mike on the side, splashed more beer on them both. Even though Luke and Conelli had arrived beside them, the car was being rocked with mounting violence. The crowd's chant shifted more and more from "Down with Microvac!" to "Break the machine!"

The driver had cut the engine, and it took McGowan a few seconds to get the car started. The model had a fluid drive with no clutch, and he put his foot hard on both brake pedal and accelerator, racing the engine with the car standing still. The engine's roar helped clear a few inches in front of the car. Waskey and the policeman opened small spaces before both front fenders. McGowan let up on the brake slightly to ease the car forward with the engine still loudly racing.

Waskey watched the car inch forward as, with polite words, he pushed his muscles against the crowd. This was the crucial instant. If the crowd's wrath did not rise over the breaking point as the car started to move, they should be all right. By luck, the cop on the other fender knew his stuff. He pushed the crowd back good-naturedly, not showing his tension by swearing or swinging. With one hand on the fender, Waskey shoved out into the people like a swimmer towing a drowning man. The hostility of the crowd rose around him like a nightmare wall, higher and higher and higher. Still the car crawled forward, the crowd moving with it like an army of ants around a tiny, slow-moving piece of sugar.

They reached the police car in front, still going at an inching walk. "Tight!" yelled Waskey back over the headlights to McGowan.

McGowan swung to the left slightly, and the convertible eased by the police car with less than an inch to spare, scraping the hangers-on off that side of Mike's car. With the length of the police car as a bulwark on the left, Waskey added his weight for a few seconds to the cop's side to break the right farther open. The headlights began to show open space between people and car. Luke hauled off two people hanging on the back. Waskey shoved back to the left side. They rounded the police car, moving at a dog trot, and picked up speed. Now only a few scattered groups blocked the road in front.

"Take it away, Mac!" Waskey and the cop leaped back. McGowan accelerated and took off down the road, followed by the yelling crowd of students and toughs, who raced past Waskey and the cop without pausing. Disregarding a red light, McGowan spurted off the campus road onto the main street. From the other side of the campus came the wail of a police siren. Reinforcements, called for over the patrol-car radio, were finally arriving.

"Thanks," said Waskey to the cop.

"Lucky," said the cop.

Microvac flew back to East Virginia the next day, the cries of "Break the machine" still oscillating in its memory circuits. En route, it reanalyzed the problems of human irrationality. On arrival it briefly exchanged information with Repcal I on this subject and on the creation of the new machines. Then it began to marshal its strength for the convention, calling and writing followers and fence-sitters around the country. Politics, Microvac realized, were even more important to machines than it had first thought.

CHAPTER SIX

THE OPENING HOUR OF THE DEMLICAN CONVENTION WAS
still five days away. The candidates and their chief managers had not yet reached Chicago, nor had that vast
army of assistant spear-carriers, bagmen, hinge-oilers,
suitcase-openers, and slightly soiled odd-jobbers that
exists close to political lords. The amateurs and citizens' groups that blossom in a presidential year—
feared by professionals, essential to the candidate—
had not yet come to add color to the crowds. But
already restaurant and elevator service had begun to
break down. Baggy-eyed professionals bounded jovially
about hotel corridors, whispered in corners, bought
plastic buttons, hired bands for spontaneous demon-
strations, ransacked model agencies for lush-looking volunteers, supervised phone installations, lined up blocks
of hotel rooms, and bickered endlessly with one another. Chicago was warming up for a hot convention.

Across the vast reaches of America, interest in politics was rising. The baseball season was slow, summer
television worse than usual, the crop of August mur-
ders uninspired. There was nothing to fall back on but
politics. Besides, while Admiral Foster Growley obviously had the Repicrat nomination sewed up, all signs
pointed to a wide-open Demlican convention.

There was general disagreement as to the Demlican

favorite. Dangle's manager, Bill Sprague, insisted his candidate would be in on the first or second ballot. Mc-Gowan, as befits the handler of a later starter, prophesied Microvac on an early ballot. The press found Microvac's slightly more impressive showing as a vote-getter offset by Dangle's firm control over the party machinery and alliance with powerful senators and congressmen. On the whole, it looked like Dangle. But no matter whom a reporter picked, he always hastened to add, "It could go either way."

Chief of Microvac's advance men in Chicago was the new assistant campaign manager, a dapper Kentuckian named Baird Tillsman. Tillsman, an ex-Sunday School teacher with the brains and morals of a second-rate traveling corset salesman, had an airtight political organization and controlled the Governor of Kentucky. Joe Waskey had been sent along to do Tillsman's work and keep him happy.

Waskey was having his troubles. He sat in his small office, a hotel room monastically bare of any furniture save a desk, two phones, and two chairs, facing a key lieutenant, a huge pear-shaped man who surrounded rather than sat on his chair.

"I seen precinct fights run better than this campaign." The lieutenant waved a fist viciously in the air. "How come we gotta put up with this guy Tillsman?"

"He's got the Governor of Kentucky, and that means the Kentucky delegation, in his pocket. I know it don't seem possible, but then you never met the Governor of Kentucky. To keep Kentucky, we got to keep Tillsman —and keep him high up."

"It ain't hardly worth it. Say, why's he always callin' you 'Colonel'—'Colonel' this and 'Colonel' that?"

"McGowan's idea. He figured Tillsman's the simple type of crumb who'd be impressed by a colonel. So he introduced me to him as 'Colonel.' It don't help much. How you makin' out down there at the station?"

"Pretty good. My guys are demonstratin' in front of every incomin' train, with big Microvac banners. Dey've kept Dangle's guys so far away from that station dey can't see it wid a telescope. I'm goin' to need tree hundred more clams for the job."

"Three hundred!" Waskey sounded like a Packard salesman being offered a Model T in full payment for a new convertible. "What've you got down there? Entertainers straight from Broadway? A sixty-piece all-girl orchestra ridin' elephants nude? I could buy the vote of every lousy delegate gettin' off at the North Station for three hundred."

"Flip ya! You know this ain't our town. You're startin' to sound like that jerk Tillsman. I've kept Dangle's guys out of the station for two days." The huge pear-shaped man heaved himself up and waddled toward Joe's desk with the sway of a menacing bulldog. "Tree hundred!" He brought a cigar out of an inside pocket, bit the end off, and spat it across the room with violence; the end made a distinct *pap* over the noise of the air conditioning as it hit the window, and stuck for a few seconds before dropping to the floor. He took a kitchen match out of an inside pocket and dragged it across the underside of Joe's desk top.

"Two-fifty," said Waskey, motionless.

"Okay. Two-fifty. How cheap can you get."

Waskey reached into the right-hand drawer of his desk, selected a fat envelope, and slipped off the elastic. He took out a sheaf of tens and counted off twenty-five bills with the speedy unconcern of a racetrack teller. "Here. See if your guys can get some Microvac buttons on the porters out at the airport before the boss comes in tomorrow. I could spare some more to show everyone the little guys in the world are for Microvac."

"Okay, Joey." The huge bulk headed for the door. "Take it easy."

Waskey walked over to the connecting door of his hotel room and stuck his head through. "Two-fifty, North Station, Jimmy Wongo, sweetheart," he intoned expressionlessly at the *saftig*, slightly pockmarked girl behind a small desk. "You gotten McGowan yet?"

"If I'd gotten him don't you think I'd let you know? Say, Joey, can I see you a second?"

"Sure. Come in."

"What's with this Kay in our other office?"

"She's goin' to be a phone operator soon as they get the big board set up. Needed somethin' to do till then. McGowan sent her up from East Virginia. Why? Did you think she went with me?"

"I didn't know. She keeps that office full of guys. I even saw her talking to Dolan."

"A reporter, near this suite? I'll take care of that. Thanks."

"Okay, Joey. Say, how about bringing out my boy friend? You got every **other** bum in America on your payroll."

"You're out here to work, sweetheart. Now keep tryin' McGowan."

Waskey looked out his window at the little sailboats on Lake Michigan. He wondered if a sailboat was tippy like a canoe, or if you could fool around with a girl in it. Well, he wouldn't find out this trip. What the hell was he knocking himself out for Microvac for anyway? Mike was a nice guy; he'd run well in Jersey. But this two-and-three-in-the-morning stuff and going to bed so tired you couldn't have fun! Murder. And where did it get you? All he was doing was missing night law school. Until he made that, he wouldn't have his union card for the big dough. The phone rang.

"Drummond," said the girl.

"Good, I'll take him." Ed Drummond, an Ohio boxing commissioner, was in charge of one of Waskey's more difficult projects: finding a boxer called Dangle, scheduling him into Chicago, and getting him knocked out. Waskey figured the news that a Dangle had been knocked out in Chicago would give the Microvac bandwagon a big shove.

Drummond had found a Dangle on the Pacific Coast and got him a Chicago match with one Kid Wachusettes, but the fix was getting expensive. As they were checking the details, the girl looked in to say that McGowan was on. Waskey cut off Drummond and grabbed the other phone.

"Mac? Mac? Hi. Oh, most things are goin' okay. Yeah, a couple of things are goin' pretty well. But I got some more trouble. Listen to this.

"Remember you phoned in two days ago to say that

you and Microvac had gotten a commitment out of the leaders of the Maryland delegation? That Maryland would go for Microvac? And Tillsman insisted on makin' the announcement out here? Well, we finally got the press release out today, and listen to how it reads.

" 'From the Campaign Office of Baird G. Tillsman.

" 'Baird G. Tillsman, Kentucky National Committeeman, today made the following dramatic announcement. Mr. Tillsman analyzed a new political trend for the press as follows:

" ' "I have seen a great deal of politics," Mr. Baird G. Tillsman said in a fighting statement, "but I have never seen such a trend as the one going at present. All over America people are following the lead of the Kentucky delegation led by Baird G. Tillsman and switching to a fighting candidate in the great tradition. Today it was Maryland that swung into line. Who knows what state it will be tomorrow, as other great organizations rush to get into line behind Microvac, a proven winner." '

"I told him I thought he was spellin' 'Microvac' wrong. He was spellin' it 'Tillsman.' "

"Now, look." McGowan's voice was severe over the phone. "Joe, I've got enough troubles without you and him squabbling. I know he's a bum. You know he's a bum. But I sent you up there to get along with him. What'd you let him issue this release for?"

"How can you stop a guy who's your boss from issuin' a release he wants to?"

"Okay. We'll issue 'em from here from now on. You having any other trouble?"

"Well, you ain't goin' to like this either. He's been cancelin' a lot of your projects. He canceled that big block of hotel rooms you were holdin' over at the Plaza. Now he's freezin' out our assistant chairman from California, who knows his stuff. He canceled my contracts for girls to hand out buttons in the other hotels—claims he can get some for less. Only I seen his girls. They couldn't pin a button on a blind man. I've hired a few from New York to come out anyway so at least the press can get some pictures."

"He canceled those hotel rooms? Doesn't he know they're scarcer than uranium?" Now McGowan was shouting. "I guess I'd better get out there tomorrow. I can leave Luke back here with Microvac."

Waskey smiled. Getting McGowan out to Chicago was the most important thing he had done all day.

While Waskey set up the Chicago headquarters, Microvac was spending its last few days in East Virginia almost continuously on the telephone. There were occasional pauses to dictate press bulletins, shake hands with important visitors, or pass on strategy to aides. But these were minor interruptions in the twenty-four-hour round of calls. The machine was influencing people and gathering its forces all over America.

Microvac, with only two tubes working on phoning, realized that other critical details were going unattended. The headquarters was burgeoning. There were arguments to settle, lieutenants to select, letters to answer, reporters to see. But the machine could do only two things at once, and, even though it handled two phones day and night, the backlog of important calls increased. The logical solution was to train Repcal I and Repcal II, just completed, to handle phone calls. Microvac could teach the two everything it knew about politics in seven minutes—there were great advantages in being able to bypass the imperfections of language and communicate electronically. But Microvac rejected this solution. The danger of discovery was too great.

Privately, it did put Repcal I to work on one vital problem—creating a dollar reserve. Bilfer, with a liberal assist from McGowan and Microvac, had raised enough money for an average primary campaign. But Dangle's headquarters, skillfully financed by Matchelder, still outspent them two to one. Waskey's operations, in particular, were always in the red. And McGowan had alarming reports that Kansas, once hot for Microvac, was cooling off under a steady stream of cold Dangle cash.

Microvac restudied everything it knew about economics, money supply, printing, paper texture, and the financial structure of the United States. The machine even had a brief chat with Waskey on fixing horse races, but rejected this idea as technically non-feasible on short notice. Finally it arrived at the easiest logical solution and turned the execution over to Repcal I.

Microvac was handling two phones when McGowan looked in before leaving for Chicago. On the right-hand phone it was wooing a leader of the Cooperative Dairy Farmers Milk Conference. The left side soothed a shipping owner worried about falling profits.

"I can assure you the problem of the dairy farmer receives my closest attention," the right side of the machine's mouth said smoothly. "I have had Ole Swenson advising me on it for some time. You didn't know that? Ole and I are firm friends. I understand that he is a friend of yours. Aren't you the Masterson he was telling me about who developed the enriched-vitamin-feeding method to produce more milk? That was quite a method." (It was, too. The cows died from swollen tongues.)

There was a long pause on Microvac's right while the machine listened to details of the government milk-purchase program the Dairy Farmers Cooperative desired. The program had the cows practically squirting five-dollar bills directly into the milk pails. "Fine," Microvac commented. "Very interesting. Fine. An unusual idea in its grasp and sweep of essentials. Letting the milk flow directly into the Treasury Department to simplify bookkeeping is indeed a new approach. I'd be interested to hear more details when I see you in Chicago. Thank you for calling. I'm counting on your help. And don't worry, I'll take care of your hotel room. Good-by."

Meanwhile the left side of Mike's mouth was making reassuring noises about "the undergirding of the American economy, the American Merchant Marine." McGowan noticed that three more calls were being held on the automatic switchboard outside Microvac's room. As the machine put down the right-hand phone he said, "I'm off to Chicago."

Microvac waved its right hand. The right side of its mouth said, "Don't let Tillsman get you down." The left side continued to make cooing noises about United States bottoms. McGowan smiled, waved in his turn, and left.

McGowan arrived quietly in Chicago, walked into an airport pay-phone booth, and dialed Microvac's headquarters. He recognized Kay's voice. McGowan always made sure that crucial people like telephone operators were loyal to him, and when Kay had asked if she could go to Chicago, he had immediately said yes.

'This is McGowan, Kay. I'd like to talk to Waskey."

"Oh, Mr. McGowan, Mr. Tillsman told me to have you connected with him as soon as you called."

"Just forget it and let me have Waskey. Don't tell Tillsman I called." He chatted briefly with Waskey and then drove on into town, feeling the old fire of battle rise in him as it always did when he approached a convention city.

Five minutes after McGowan had reached his hotel, Tillsman was swarming all over him, reporting on the excellent job he, Tillsman, had been doing. McGowan could cheerfully have strangled him, but then he would have lost Kentucky, so he patted Tillsman on the back and heaped congratulations on his slicked head. By the end of the day he had undone some of Tillsman's major tangles.

There was the little matter of the Sheriff's Palomino Posse from Bluegrass, Kentucky. The men and their twelve horses were being quartered in Chicago at Microvac's expense. "Why," Tillsman informed McGowan with surprise when he realized that his genius was being questioned, "that organization is not only famous in Kentucky but is beloved by horse lovers and sheriffs throughout the whole of America. You wouldn't want me to send them back." There was a long pause. "Why, if word leaked out those hosses were returning, people everywhere would be saying Microvac is through."

"If the word gets out to the press that Microvac is keeping twelve horses, they'll make sure he's through. Now look, Baird, Microvac is a very precise machine, and he knows horses don't vote. You get them out of town tomorrow, and we'll pay their freight back. Otherwise they're going back on their own." McGowan figured that by offering to pay their fare back he could get the horses out of town gracefully before they and their riders ate their way through the entire convention treasury.

"Now"—McGowan pulled out of his pocket one of the innumerable small slips of paper he always carried—"here is another one Mike's accountants passed on to me to ask you about: one hundred Indian war bonnets (de luxe), one thousand five hundred dollars. What did we get scalped on that one for?"

"Oh, those are very important."

"They cost like it." There was a pause that grew longer. "What are they for?"

"Lulu Belle would know."

"Who?"

"Lulu Belle Winston, my secretary. Used to be Joe Wumpardale's secretary. Everybody knows her in the Southwest. She's a grand girl. She keeps track of things like that."

"Good. Let's ask her."

Lulu Belle was nowhere to be found. This was fine, as it enabled Tillsman to transfer his ire from McGowan—someone above him—to Lulu Belle—someone below him—and made McGowan's task of cracking down on expenditures easier. By early the next morning he had got most of the financial control of the headquarters out of Tillsman's hands and into his own. There had never been any doubt that he could do this, since the money was Microvac's to begin with, and Microvac would have backed him in a showdown. But by spending a whole day he had saved Kentucky for Microvac. Once the convention was over, they could dump Tillsman.

With Tillsman off his neck, McGowan began the crucial job of juggling Vice Presidents. Texas, Pennsylvania, and Indiana all had favorite sons with vice-presidential ambitions. Microvac's strategy was to indicate to each man that he was the machine's first and only choice, if he would deliver his state. The clearness of the indication was a point of disagreement between Microvac and McGowan. McGowan felt that the unwritten rules of politics prohibited more than a firm indication. Microvac insisted on an outright promise to each. Both agreed that the young, hustling Mayor of Detroit, George Churpwell, would be the best Vice President on a Microvac ticket. But Dangle held Michigan solidly, so there was no gain in letting that out until Microvac was nominated.

Late that evening, in his plush rococo suite, McGowan held a conference with two key members of the Indiana delegation. An aide poured coffee while McGowan padded about the room, lighting and grinding out cigarettes.

The talk was about Whitey Bird, Indiana's favorite son. The larger of the two delegates extolled his virtues.

"We think a lot of Whitey in Indiana. He's been a great, forward-looking governor. There's hardly a Repicrat dares run for office."

"I know Whitey well. He would undoubtedly add great strength to any ticket he is on. I know from personal knowledge that Microvac is fond of him—very fond." McGowan was all earnest accord. "Mike wants to see Whitey right away, as soon as he gets to Chicago. Now, I don't want any rumors started. You and I know what rumors are. They're vicious things—vicious things. So why don't you just bring Whitey in quietly? After they meet we can probably get together and take care of a few practical details."

"Now, we wouldn't want to be party to any deals." The second Indiana delegate had his mouth open and was panting.

McGowan looked pained that Microvac's fondness for Whitey Bird should ever be thought of as a deal. He looked just as pained the next morning when talking with Texas delegates about their state's senior senator, and the next afternoon when discussing the Governor of Pennsylvania.

"These wiseacres that claim the Vice President isn't important don't know what they're talking about," McGowan remarked later to Waskey. "Why, you get terrific political mileage out of just a whiff of that office."

"Yeah, probably when that jerk Whitey Bird was little he used to turn to his daddy and say, 'When I grow up I want to be a Vice President.'"

Waskey too had a part in these maneuverings. He had printed up three sets of slogan buttons, each set linking Microvac's name with one of the three vice-

presidential hopefuls. The buttons bore no marks by
which their origin could be traced. The proper sets just
appeared in the rooms of delegates from Indiana, Texas,
and Pennsylvania as if dropped by pixies. To be caught
printing buttons boosting three separate Vice Presidents on Microvac's ticket would have embarrassed
even Waskey.

Baird Tillsman was also made part of the strategy.
McGowan told him that there had been a deal, but
wouldn't tell him with whom, and swore him to secrecy.
Tillsman, to prove he was in Microvac's confidence,
rushed around and told the press, and every delegate he
happened to see, that a deal had been made. This made
the three hopefuls feel that things were set, and left the
machine, Luke, and McGowan free to deny everything.

Microvac, Luke, Conelli, two secretaries, the inevitable mimeograph machine, and ten members of the
press who were covering the candidate flew to Chicago
in a chartered plane. Fellows, silently hatching Plan C
for Chicago, came along too, with the machine's extra
set of batteries. The main war party was arriving.

Luke corralled the reporters for a chat as the plane
raced westward. "Microvac and I were just talking
about this convention, and I thought you might like a
quick fill on some of the machine's thinking on Chicago."

"We sure would, Luke. Anything you can give us."
The reporters crowded close to hear Luke above the roar
of the plane.

"The important thing to remember about everything

Microvac will do at Chicago is that Microvac is in this campaign as a matter of principle. He is a fighter, and he intends to fight. But it's going to be a fight on principle. The vast majority of the delegates who will be at the convention are men of principle. Principles, ideas, victory—these are the important things to them. California and his other primary victories show that Microvac is the one man who can beat Admiral Growley. Now Microvac's aim at this convention is to strengthen the great principles upon which the Demlican party was founded. A return to principle, plus Microvac's nomination, is certain to produce victory in November."

"Okay. Let's cut this general stuff and get down to specifics," said one of the reporters, lugubriously moving a large pencil across the pages of a tiny notebook. "Who does Microvac want for Vice President?"

"Now here's another area where principle is at work," Luke replied with force. "Microvac specifically laid down to his top staff before they went to Chicago, and I was there, that there were to be no deals on the Vice Presidency. We have no list, we have no favorite few, we have no commitments. We have just one requirement for the job—ability. This may be poor politics, but it's good for the country, and that's the way we are going to run the show at Chicago."

"Would the senior senator from Texas fill the requirement of ability?" a reporter asked.

"The senior senator from Texas is acknowledged to be a very able man."

"How about the Indiana Governor, Whitey Bird?"

"Everyone knows Whitey Bird's outstanding record."

"How about Whistling Willie Gasper, the junior senator from Kentucky?" asked another, naming one of the Senate's outstanding drunken boneheads.

"There is no point in trying to get me to run down a list of names one by one. Any man of outstanding ability is acceptable. Let's leave it at that, since that's the way it is. Now, how about a drink? How about it? We have a long, hard week ahead of us, fighting for principle against those political cutthroats Dangle has gathered around him with crude promises of patronage and cash."

To the clink of glasses, Microvac raced on toward Chicago at four hundred miles an hour for the final, crucial days of the fight with Dangle.

CHAPTER SEVEN

BRYANT W. DANGLE'S HEADQUARTERS WERE FAR FROM
inactive. Under Matchelder's skillful financial direction,
there was money to burn—if burning money would
have helped. The TV commercials were fast-paced, the
staff scrubbed, the strategy conferences animated, the
headquarters adorned with powerful representatives and
senators, and the reporters covering the campaign were
enthusiastically for Dangle. Political maneuvers were
astutely plotted and piloted by Bill Sprague, a tough,
genial organizer. An attractive group of high-minded
volunteers who regarded Microvac as a repetitive au-
tomaton had rallied to Dangle, filling his hotel rooms
with intellectual ferment. His wife, while still not able
to do much politicking, was in town, helping him appear more relaxed. More important, Dangle held the
votes of New York, Ohio, Florida, Michigan, Illinois,
and a good part of the Solid South.

Outside his headquarters, Dangle had a second pow-
erhouse of reserve strength in the supposedly neutral
Demlican National Committee, solidly controlled by
his and Bill Sprague's friends. Florence Goldrush, co-
director of the committee, was a particularly effective
ally.

"I just heard, dear"—her voice, combined of equal
parts of honey and lye, rolled into her pink phone—

"that you were organizing something called the 'College Women for Microvac.' . . . I know, but I get around, dear, and I hear things. Now do you really think that's wise? . . . I know, dear, I mean really wise. . . . Of course I'm neutral, dear." She looked across at the two middle-aged ladies opposite her, wearing Dangle buttons, and cracked the pancake on her face into her conception of a smile. "Well, I certainly would hate to make a mistake, dear, if I were you. These before-convention commitments are dangerous; they have a way of being remembered. . . . Aren't you a bit uneasy, dear, as if your slip was showing? . . . I know you're for Microvac, dearie, but the machine doesn't have a chance. . . . No, he doesn't. I know what's going on, and he doesn't. . . . I'd hate to see Adelaide or some other woman get the nod as Women's Division Director in your state just because you abandoned your usual common sense. . . . Oh, no, dear, I'm not hinting anything. Just called you up for a friendly chat.. . . . Well, thank you, and same to you. Good-by."

She turned to the two women wearing Dangle buttons. "God! What a fat, stupid cow that Helen Worth is! Wants to organize college women for Microvac. I could kill her. Now, dears, don't you two worry about your problem. I'll find some television time somewhere for you to appear and talk about your cute Aprons for Demlicans drive. Of course you'll mention all those cute Dangle aprons—not that I'll know anything about it. Ha-ha." A laugh to chill the blood of an avaricious tarantula emerged from between her parted lips, while her face remained expressionless. "Well, you'll both have to pardon me now. I have to run and do a little errand for the Chairman." She rose briskly from behind her desk, pulled down the jacket of her tailored suit with the decisive tug of a trainer cinching up a steeplechaser, and grasped the hands of the waiting ladies. "Come in and see me again after you've elected Dangle. Good-by."

After she had departed, the two large Midwestern ladies at whom she had been monologuing slowly brought their mouths together. Then one said, "Did you see Flo's cute little hat? I've one almost like it myself; I bought it right here in Chicago. Ben and I came here on a trip last year."

"Whose cute hat?" The other was still a bit overcome by the presence of the great.

"Flo—Florence Goldrush. I always call her Flo. We've known each other for—well, I'd better not say how long." A girlish giggle flicked at her solid frame. "Flo knows how to get what she wants out of men politicians."

"She seems mighty sure our man Bryant is going to end up the winner."

"She knows. If she says so, it's probably been all fixed already. That's the way things are in politics, you know. Well, let's go find the girls and get them ready for television. My, won't my Ben be surprised!" The two gave a final look at themselves in Florence's large office mirror and, evidently reassured at finding their hats on their heads, moved from the room with sexless, ground-covering strides.

Florence was already gesticulating in the Chairman's office. He was talking to two key delegates, but that did not bother her. She had come in through his private

side door, shut it firmly behind her, and walked over to
introduce herself to the two men, waiting rather point-
edly for the second of them to rise. She then wheeled,
apologized for interrupting, and launched forth with
her new plan for sinking Microvac.

She ended by lecturing the two delegates on why all
women were for Dangle. Then she left by the Chairman's front door—the more people who saw you going
out of important places, the better. As the press so
often remarked, control of the party machinery was
important.

Shortly after midnight, Kay and Fellows sat on Kay's
hotel-room bed, drinking Scotch and tap water without
ice. There was no other place to sit in the narrow room,
for the one small chair was piled high with boxes. Kay
had been shopping.

"I don't know what's going to happen when everyone gets here. The stores are just too crowded for words
as it is."

"Everyone should be here by now. The voting is only
five days away."

"That switchboard can't get any worse. We're going
mad in there now. Politics is crazy—I called the same
man flying the Pacific three times this afternoon. And
that Joe Waskey, I'm glad I'm away from him. He's too
tough."

"I've never been able to figure out just what he does."

"Proffy, he'll do anything. The other day he got some
police badges forged. They put a nun's fingerprint on
them so they couldn't be traced. They're going to use
them to take over the convention floor."

"They couldn't have done that. You were being kidded."

"They didn't know I was listening."

"He should be ashamed."

"Oh, Proffy, you're the only thing I like about this campaign—you, and being in Chicago. You're sweet. Nobody around here is ashamed, including me. Look what I bought during lunch."

She took off her wrapper and went over to open one of the boxes on the chair. Fellows watched, fascinated, as she shook out a dress.

"Gosh, after following Microvac around all day and assembling voting data, all I can do is sit here and watch. We should be back at East Virginia."

Kay opened the bathroom door to view herself in its full-length mirror. "It may be a bit short." She turned halfway round tentatively.

"It looks perfect to me." Fellows lay back against the wall and closed his eyes. He was so comfortable here; in spite of where he was, he almost fell asleep. In another three and a half hours he would have to go and take care of Microvac. "If I ever fall asleep here, be sure and wake me at four thirty. I plug Microvac in at four forty-five each morning."

Kay picked up her drink and sat down on the bed beside him. "Do what?"

"At four forty-five I plug Microvac in to a high-speed teleprinter so he can teleprint orders for the staff and dictate letters and everything. The machine does a day's writing in about half an hour."

Kay yawned and sighed. "Well, I'm just a phone operator. Of course, I guess I hope Microvac wins, but

some of the things he's doing don't seem right— Hey!
I may decide to take this dress back."

At four forty-five, Fellows plugged Microvac in to the
teleprinter that was set up in an inside room in the
machine's suite. With the phone stilled and no callers
allowed, this was the one time of the day when Microvac permitted itself superhuman efficiency. The high-
speed teletype keys started with a whirr:

McGowan—see Halstead Smith and have him
threaten to remove all his liquor advertising from Ten-
nessee papers unless we are supported.

Waskey—stop paying for Delegate J. V. Burham's
girls. He has produced no delegates, and we need a
little discipline in Oregon.

Waskey—make sure that head of the Drivers' Union
calls the following delegates. [Then followed a lengthy
list with addresses and phone number.] Make sure I
learn of the reaction of each. Try and get them to sug-
gest other names to call. Check these names with me.

Conelli—tell the Joy Wagon not to start releasing
lightning bolts until after 7:30 a.m. It is waking too
many people up, and this makes them mad.

Secretary—send following telegram to Governor Har-
rison of East Virginia: "Delighted to learn that you
consider stand of your delegation and yourself still open.
If elected I pledge I will so act that history will say
that by God's grace East Virginia finally received her
full share of federal aid. This aid will be distributed before your re-election campaign. I certainly would be
proud to have the support of a man of your high caliber
who is fighting for the same great principles and lofty
ideals as myself."

Conelli—The governor of East Virginia is completely
ruled by his wife. Have one of our handsome young
volunteers meet the train to look after her bags. Send

flowers to her room from me with the following card: "A small token of thanks for a very happy time in your gracious home." Have handsome volunteer take the governor's wife to the ball game tonight. She doesn't drink.

Bilfer—have Hodgkins, that banker friend of yours with East Virginia interests, call Mr. George Tattle of Greenhedge, East Virginia, and hint that his farm land will become an important reservoir and be bought from him at a high price under the Microvac scheme for improving East Virginia. Hodgkins is younger brother of East Virginia's governor's wife. This should have priority of your very valuable time.

For an hour and three-quarters the messages clacked out at electronic-impulse speed. At six thirty Fellows, who had been snatching some sleep outside Microvac's door, where he was stationed to make certain that no one came in, withdrew the complex teletype circuit plug from its small hole in the machine's base. Then, a trifle groggily, he began changing the batteries.

During battery change, Microvac no longer had a few moments of darkness while the new batteries were being installed. Now the old batteries were lifted out still attached to the power cord. The new batteries were then placed in the carrying case just above the tracks, and connected to an alternate set of wires. Microvac itself tested the new batteries' potency before throwing an internal switch to change the power supply. After this the old batteries were disconnected. The machine had gained this security refinement with no visible change in its appearance.

Microvac rolled into the outer rooms of its suite to greet the first shift of secretaries, who were just arriving at quarter of seven. Handing them the long roll of tele-typed instructions, it wished them a cheerful good morning and thanked them for being on the job so early. It then went to its inner rooms to telephone, and to scan about twenty key newspapers.

Before the day had really started, one of the first simple phone calls trapped the machine. The operator reported that Congressman Clogg, an important figure in the civil rights picture, was on the line. But, instead of Clogg's clipped tones, an uncontrolled feminine voice rang in the machine's ear with the wild enthusiasm of the ardent past sanity.

"Whooooo, Mr. Microvac, I am so glad to talk to you at last. You will forgive my little joke at being the congressman, won't you? You know, your staff has just no idea how to make you a winner. I've been calling and calling, but they won't let me unfurl my banner over you—the banner I made for you at no cost to yourself. No, Mr. Microvac, at no cost to yourself. And yet I sense—I have remarkable senses, Mr. Microvac—that they are deliberately keeping me away. But isn't that ever the way in the world when the giver comes full-handed with thrice-blessed alms?"

"Ever so," murmured the right-hand side of Micro-vac's mouth sympathetically.

"Ah, Mr. Microvac, you thrill me. You thrill my mother, Mrs. Helen Claggett—though she can't see or hear since her stroke, poor dearest soul. Whenever I tell her about you, I can see she's thrilled. I am Nora Clag-gett. I am *the* Nora Claggett, who has the Microvac banner. It's right here in Chicago, Mr. Microvac. I brought your banner here with me. Oh, I can see what you are thinking, but I'm not going to charge you, Mr. Microvac. I've spent my own money."

"How kind." While Miss Claggett went on about the wonders of her banner, the left side of Microvac's mouth finished off its call and got the operator to interrupt the right line and get Miss Claggett off. For the machine, the day returned briefly to normal. Miss Claggett's life went back to normal too. Her constant calls were passed from junior staff member to junior staff member.

At eight Microvac's day went completely off schedule. Four Illinois delegates arrived for breakfast with the machine at the same moment that Baird Tillsman phoned. The four delegates were crucial. There was a chance that they might switch from Dangle. This break in a key state would dump politically hot particles over the convention. Microvac figured it could deal with Tillsman rapidly, then charm the delegates.

But Tillsman was far too upset to be rapid. He had a host of real and imagined woes. Microvac tried to shut him up by asking repeatedly how he was getting on with Missouri. Missouri was a hopeless state, completely for Dangle. McGowan had told Tillsman to work on it, realizing that he could do no harm there.

Tillsman wound on with problem after problem. "I don't know what McGowan's doing, Microvac. Sometimes it don't seem to me like he can really follow through. Has he told you Bill Finney would like to see you?"

"Who?"

"Bill Finney from Clarksberg, Kentucky."

"But I've already seen him once, and he's only an

alternate. Besides, he's one of your boys. We've got him."

"Yes, I know, but Bill would like to see you again and bring a few friends. He's got some very powerful friends."

"Who are these friends?"

"Well, I don't exactly know now just which ones he has in mind as of this moment for the first meeting. Lulu Belle hasn't given me the list. But here's the way I figure it should be handled."

"Why don't you find out who the friends are and call me back?"

But Tillsman was riveted to the phone. Microvac even considered rudeness, but this might have jeopardized Kentucky. Only by inviting Tillsman in for a real chat that evening did it finally manage to end the conversation.

By then the breakfast was shot. The delegates were scattered about Microvac's large living room, mumbling at one another, their attitudes as congealed as their half-eaten eggs. As Microvac started to turn on its well-machined charm, a secretary bustled in with the possessive air of those close to the great, to say Whitey Bird was on the phone. At the same moment Conelli slid through a side door to whisper that the presidents of the Committee for a More Beautiful Montana and the Committee for a More Beautiful Arizona were outside. These two men controlled the mining lobby and should be seen immediately.

Microvac paused in the center of the room. It had three absolutely vital tasks to do at once. Its tubes calculated quickly. The mining lobbyists would have to wait, the Illinois delegates must be passed on to McGowan, and Whitey Bird must be dealt with first. When machines ran the government, politics would progress in a predictable pattern.

Microvac apologized to the four Illinois delegates for not having been able to spend more time with them and buzzed for Conelli to take them to McGowan. Even the machine's parting handshake went wrong. Two of the delegates were in the middle of lighting their after-breakfast cigars. This is the one moment at which a politician cannot instantly grab an outstretched hand. Failure in this particular flooded the men with acute embarrassment, as if they had been Western heroes late on the draw. Unless McGowan produced a miracle, the Illinois delegates weren't going to switch.

"Where's Luke?" A static bark came from Microvac as the machine rolled to the phone.

"Here." Another door of the suite popped open.

"Look, Luke. Get that ass, Tillsman, on the television tonight and tell me the time. Make sure he's really on and can't get off. I'll invite him to see me at the time he's on the program, and that will get me out of having to see him. And keep those two mine lobbyists from the Committees for a More Beautiful Montana and Arizona happy. Lou Sorenson, the guy from Montana, breeds prize boxers."

Microvac reached the phone. Whitey Bird had heard rumors that he was no longer the machine's only candidate for Vice President. Microvac spent ten minutes reassuring him in detail. Then the machine rolled into another room in its suite to deal with the mining lobby.

By the time the two leaders of the mining lobby had

left, Microvac was ten minutes late for a Wisconsin caucus in a hotel on the other side of town. Conelli got an
elevator to come directly to the machine's floor. A five-
man phalanx of union organizers from the Rock Workers, and vacationing Jersey City Riot Squad cops, made
a flying wedge around Microvac and Luke and headed
down the corridor. Behind came Conelli with a roll of
bills to smooth the way where muscle failed. The photographers and reporters doomed by their editors to follow Microvac twenty-four hours a day took off also,
fighting through the crowd that surged in to catch a
glimpse of the famous machine.

Outside the hotel three limousines, led by a police
car, waited for Microvac. The mayor of Chicago, a
strong Dangle man, did not particularly want to supply
the police car, but neither did he want nothing but a
large horse laugh when he came to Washington to ask
for a federal handout if Microvac won the election.
Dangle had four police cars and a motorcycle escort.
The mayor knew the difference between political safety
and neutrality.

A crowd of curious pressed round Mike's car as it
drew up at the new hotel. The phalanx formed at the
door. With a rush two of the phalanx helped the machine up the steps, and they swung through the hotel
lobby toward the elevators.

"Where are we going?" yelled the lead bodyguard.

"The Wisconsin caucus in the Green Room, third
floor," Luke shouted back.

They arrived at the elevators. There was a half-block
line before the doors. The crowd began to compress
about the phalanx and machine.

Conelli, who had friends in every hotel in Chicago, grabbed a bell captain. "Hey, Paul, take us to the Green Room in the freight elevator."

"This way, sir."

"This way," yelled Conelli. The phalanx wheeled in the new direction, cutting a swath like a line of Scythian. chariots. A hotel policeman guarding the swinging-door entrance to the service elevators was hipped into a potted palm. Slapping the leaves from his face, he gave a shout and started after Microvac. Conelli's hand poked out from behind the closing swing door and stopped him cold with a five.

Along the back corridors of the third floor the phalanx twisted and jogged, picking up speed behind the bell captain. Ahead appeared a jam of people clustered around a door. With a cry of "Sorry, mac," the phalanx burst through, momentum carrying it and the machine a good way into the room. Reporters accordioned in after Microvac like straphangers on a suddenly stalled subway.

The phalanx untangled itself from the chairs in front of a yogurt-and-daiquiri-fed model sashaying down a runway. "And now a forest-green creation of soft molded chiffon, draped enticingly for formal evening wear," a dulcet voice echoed over the room's loudspeakers. One of the phalanx let out a piercing whistle of appreciation.

"The Green Room," announced the bell captain in stentorian tones.

"Pardon, to see Madame Hugo's Fall Showing you must have ze ticket," a female fashion executive shrieked from the door.

"Hurrah! Hurrah! And jubilee! I have found you!

Oh, Mr. Microvac!" A disheveled elderly lady in the back of the room lurched toward the machine. In her hands she bore a nine-foot pole from whose top fluttered a gigantic green and blue pennant with a gold radio tube on it. Beneath the tube were embroidered in scarlet the words, "Prepare for Doom."

"It's me, me, Nora Claggett, and my Microvac flag." With strands of unwashed gray hair flying, the woman bore down on the phalanx, swinging her flagpole like a crusader's battle ax.

"Jesus! She could be me mudder-in-law." The front man of the phalanx quailed.

"Hey, Mr. Microvac," the photographers yelled as one man. "How about a picture with that babe on the runway?"

"Who were those two men coming out of your room just as we left?" several reporters asked.

"Oh, Wisconsin, where have you gone?" Luke covered his face with his hands.

"Luke, get that Claggett woman away before she cracks me with that pole," the machine whispered tersely.

"Hey, girls, girls, girls, over here." More models appeared, and the photographers waved their cameras aloft as bait.

"Take the mystic flag, Mr. Microvac. Oh, my machine, take the mystic flag. It's free."

"I am the most certain positeeve Madame Hugo would never approve poleeteecs in her collection."

"Aw, shove over, Auntie, and let us shoot girls who've got somethin'."

"Don't shoot—don't shoot—till we get our TV cam-

eras set up. Here comes the cable now." Two heaving
roustabouts were snaking a heavy cable across the room.
They flipped it over a line of chairs, fetching the ladies
in the next row an oily smack.

"Hands off dat cable!" they yelled crossly.

"Who did you say was with you just before we left?"
a reporter persisted.

Microvac realized that this was going to be another
political day. "Two gentlemen from the West came in
to pay their respects," it answered.

A gang of teen-agers that had been passing by in the
corridor pressed in, giggling and yelling for autographs.
The phalanx disintegrated to glam the models. An informal press conference got under way. Photographers
demanded room. Madame Hugo's female factotum
tripped over the TV cable. Miss Claggett waved her flag
aloft and burst into song, thumping her chest loudly
each time she chanted the chorus:

> "Boom, boom!
> Prepare for doom."

Conelli elbowed his way back into the room. "Wisconsin's canceled until one thirty tomorrow. They say
they told Tillsman."

By the time the machine returned to its hotel headquarters it was close to an hour late.

The headquarters to which Microvac now returned
was in a new hotel. Every three hours during the day the
machine switched headquarters in an effort to shake the
clutter of hangers-on, unemployed delegates, lobbyists,
crackpots, and minor factotums who made work all but
impossible.

At about five the phalanx began to slow, in spite of an almost continuous intake of liquid energy. Luke dropped out to watch the evening television programs and to brief reporters. Conelli went off to check a rumor that Dangle had slipped a non-union guitar-player into Microvac's hillbilly orchestra.

Microvac plowed tirelessly on, shaking hands, talking, listening, agreeing, influencing. At six thirty it held a brief strategy huddle with McGowan in the latter's suite. Even the indestructible McGowan was showing signs of wear; his shoulders sagged as if exhausted by the weight of his arms; his eyes were blurred and red like two round hunks of melting raspberry ice; the hands that plucked little pieces of notepaper from his pockets had a definite tremor. Like a miler with the end in sight, he was putting everything into his last kick.

He fished the little pieces of paper out one by one—they formed part of the ritual of his political personality. There was a disturbing report that the Demlican National Committee was doing them dirt in New Jersey. The Illinois switch delegates wanted another meeting; ten forty-five that evening was agreed on. The mining-lobby chiefs had ordered Bates Hewball, "the sheep's friend," and a few other minor delegates to switch to Microvac. Baird Tillsman had made a bad statement on water resources, and Colorado had turned sour. Tillsman had also told some delegates that Microvac would not fight against the Strong Union amendment, a plank designed to cripple labor unions.

"I wish I could think of something to do with Tillsman," Microvac remarked, its tubes barren of ideas.

"He could drop dead," said McGowan, bitterly weary.

"He could," replied Microvac, "but would we still have the Governor of Kentucky? Tillsman's deputy reportedly wants to go to Dangle."

McGowan looked up sharply. Microvac must have been joking. The machine's complete lack of facial expression sometimes confused him. Microvac saw the glance and went on quickly, reinforcing in its memory circuits the fact that logical information could not always be given to McGowan.

"How do the three vice-presidential states look to you?"

"Holding firm." Using two hands, McGowan lit a new cigarette from the end of the old. He was still unhappy about a straight promise to three men. Microvac wouldn't get much help in those states if he was nominated. But he knew Microvac had an answer to that one too. Politicians, the machine had said, got you nominated; people got you elected. He fished another slip from his pocket. "What about Oklahoma?" he asked.

"I've found the money to take care of Oklahoma, Kansas, and part of Washington."

"Just a clean, straight bribe?"

"Right," Microvac said softly.

"Have we got enough?"

"I think I'm going to be able to command some unforeseen capital."

"Where from?"

"I'd rather not say."

McGowan didn't like his candidate to keep secrets from him, but he recognized that there were some things best known to the fewest people. "You doing the whole thing yourself?" he asked a trifle suspiciously.

"Waskey is handling the buying."

McGowan shook his head. He was glad to be out of something he basically disapproved of, but annoyed that anything so important should be handled by anyone but himself. He fished a blank slip of paper from an inside pocket and made a note to ask Waskey about Oklahoma.

Microvac recognized McGowan's slight uneasiness and launched into a state-by-state summary. The machine had learned that it could always reassure Mac with a detailed analysis of events all over the convention. After about ten more minutes of political gossip, the two broke up to return to the constant rush of meeting people.

The vital political time of day was approaching—the hours between nine in the evening and three in the morning when the weak fade and the strong join in alliance. Then the small politicians, the spectators, most of the press and lobbyists retire exhausted. Freed from interruptions, the old pros, calling on inner resources of vitality, rise to deal.

These hours were peculiarly Microvac's. No fatigue poison dulled the workings of the machine's tubes. No alcohol taken in desperation to keep going fuzzed its electronic precision. No fear of exhaustion tomorrow caused it to let up for an instant today.

At eleven fifteen came the first break in the rounds of important outside callers. Carrying a small satchel, Joe Waskey slid into Microvac's suite through the connecting door to the next set of rooms, which supposedly belonged to a beer company. For half an hour the two exchanged information: reports from the delegates loyal to Microvac who were caucusing with Dangle's forces; what Dangle's wastebaskets revealed; what Waskey's girls had discovered; how much the forged police badges had cost; the number of delegates staying in hotel rooms Microvac was paying for; how best to jam the radio net Dangle had set up to control his floor strategy.

After this routine business there was a slight pause; then Microvac opened the major problem. "Have you looked into the Oklahoma situation?"

"Yes, sir."

"How much do you think we can get Oklahoma for?"

"Seven thousand. Dangle's been biddin' up the market price of Okies."

"That is high. How about Kansas?"

"Four or five. Nobody's payin' much attention to them now."

"Any price on the uncommitted Washington delegates?"

"About the same."

"The Panama Canal Zone?"

"No use wastin' any time with those guys. They're independents. They'll take your money, liquor, and women and then vote for the other guy. To hell with them. They never stay bought."

Microvac rolled over to an ornate Louis Quatorze desk in the corner of its rococo suite. "Here is thirty thousand, Joe. That should help us compete with the Dangle forces."

Waskey was enough of a philosopher to be silent in the presence of so much money. From long training, he tore the brown paper off one bundle, looked closely at the sheaves of tens, put one sheaf in his pocket, and stowed the rest in his satchel. "This should make a difference," he said with quiet intensity.

"I should tell you, Joe, and I have not and will not tell this to anyone but you: There is a small difference between this money and that normally in use. This money was not printed by the United States Government. Otherwise it is exactly the same."

In spite of his long political apprenticeship, Waskey dropped his satchel. He grabbed the sheaf of tens from his pocket as if it had just sunk large incisors into the soft flesh above his liver. He pulled two tens from the sheaf and went over to the light. Then he reached for his own wallet, drew out another ten, and placed it between the first two. Except for the controlled mechanical hum of the air-conditioner, the room was silent.

"This is good stuff. I used to know a lot of the numbers boys, and I've seen a lot of phonies. This stuff looks perfect to me."

"The paper quality is, chemically, microscopically different," replied Microvac, "but I don't think the payees will notice. If they do find out after the convention, will they admit to anyone that they received counterfeit money as a bribe from us? Understand me—I'd rather do it with real money, but we don't have enough around to compete with Dangle."

"You're sure the printer is reliable?"

"Both the printer and the paper-maker are completely beholden to me."

"Yeah," said Waskey. This meant a long-term federal rap, but somebody in the organization had to face the federal raps, and that guy, if he played it right, should have a good future. "I'll bring those states in," he said, moving toward the door with his usual quiet purpose-fulness. "There's a few other things I can do too. But from now on, Mr. Microvac, the less you know about this, the better."

"I couldn't win this one without you, Joe," said Microvac, placing a warm, fatherly hand between his shoulders.

After Waskey left, the round of regular conferences continued. At about one, Luke came to discuss press strategy for the coming day. After he left, three senior Demlican congressmen who were drafting the Strong Union amendment filed in. Conservative Demlicans were pressing to make this amendment part of the party platform. Since most of those for the amendment were for Dangle, Microvac strongly opposed it. The three congressmen had pulled a swifty. They had got Tillsman on their side and had invited him to take part in the meeting. Microvac saw Tillsman at the door and has-tened to back him out, feigning annoyance at his han-dling of Missouri.

Pushing Tillsman was not too difficult. He badly wanted to crawl into bed. Not for amorous reasons; Tillsman had that stern morality many men adopt to hide a low level of sexual vitality. A pinch or two a month, and he was happy. But he prided himself on his physique and believed he needed seven hours of sleep a night to keep his tummy flat. He had tried to attend the conference mostly through pique at the idea of being left out. Microvac's reassurance that they could have a long talk at three that morning almost made him quake visibly. Later in the day he was going to appear on two television programs that were going into Kentucky. What if he didn't look his best to his friends! He assured Microvac that he would call him if anything important came up, and that they could talk tomorrow. Microvac bade him a cheery good night.

Over two hours later the meeting between Microvac and the three congressmen broke up in complete disagreement and profuse political politeness. As the last "What an inestimable pleasure to have had the privilege of a few moments of your very valuable time" faded, the machine pivoted rapidly toward its two phones to relay its version of the stand-off conference to a series of key supporters. The next half-hour would be crucial, as each side tried to give the impression it had won.

Microvac didn't forget to ask the chief phone operator how she was feeling at this hour. "Just numb, sir, just numb; but then, that's politics. Don't you ever get tired, Mr. Microvac?"

"I'm exhausted," the machine lied.

The three congressmen made the mistake of pausing to revive themselves with a drink while they reviled the machine. Later that day Microvac's version of the Strong Union amendment was accepted by the convention.

At 4:07 a.m. Microvac moved to the ordinary typewriter in its suite. There it typed a letter to a small electronics firm, ordering a variety of complex parts to be shipped to its laboratories in East Virginia. With campaign funds, the vital business of secretly creating more machines could move rapidly. Microvac then picked up a list of critical phone calls the staff wanted made and began phoning.

At four forty-three the machine put the two phones

down, leaving a few calls still unmade. It rolled into its inner room. Professor Fellows was just arriving.

The scientist looked a bit hastily put together. Microvac's sensitive photoelectric cells recorded a definite lipstick smear on his neck, only partially hidden by his collar. The machine's memory circuits made a note to tap Fellows' phone.

Fellows plugged Microvac in to the high-speed teletypewriter. With a constant whirr of keys, terse orders and messages began to pour out. Another political day for Microvac ended and began.

Imperceptibly to those caught at the vortex, but none the less decisively, the convention was shifting away from Bryant W. Dangle. A series of minor disasters plagued the Dangle camp and kept its forces off balance. A button boosting a Dangle-Caleb ticket mysteriously appeared around Dangle headquarters. Mere mention of Senator Caleb's name was enough to cast doubt on Dangle's liberal principles. Then the Fraternal Organization of New England Psychiatrists elected Dangle "the patient we would most like to see in the White House." All over the convention delegates began drawing each other aside to murmur, "A guy that's crazy would have a hard time of it in my district." Actually Dangle, at the age of six, had been twice to see a psychiatrist to help cure a nervous stutter.

Finally, the day before Dangle planned to announce a vast federally financed power program to swing Western delegates to his side, Microvac announced the identical scheme.

"Goddamn it! There's a spy in this headquarters,"

yelled Dangle when Sprague and Matchelder brought him the newspapers with details of Microvac's Western power plan.

"I have already instructed the detective agency I am employing in this campaign to double its security efforts." Matchelder dripped the words icily.

"Right. Right," said Dangle, showing his usual leadership. "You know, this leak and that New England psychiatrist fraud smack of the work of that fellow we ran into out in California. What was his name?"

"Joseph Waskey," said Bill Sprague quietly. "I think you're right. This smells like Waskey."

"I've never heard of him," remarked Matchelder in a tone indicating that this fact alone should rid the earth of this creature forever.

"He's a bum from the docks, with a little college polish, that Microvac picked up in New Jersey. An anything-for-a-vote guy, he fits right in with Microvac-McGowan."

"He's got a spy in this headquarters," Dangle reiterated with high-pitched testiness.

Dangle was wrong. Waskey had no spy in the headquarters. He did have a friend, Stoker Swenson, who, with the help of a little of Microvac's U.S.-minted money, had gained the trash concession from Dangle's hotel. After removing the trash, Stoker and a few pals— Stoker had a wide acquaintanceship—went through the mess to see if they could find any interesting papers for their old friend Waskey. For this Stoker was paid. Then he sold the trash. For this he was paid. He kept back some of the really choice information and slipped it to a friend, who sold it to Waskey as coming from some-where else. The friend then split with Stoker. Further, everything was for cash, which meant no books. "No cut for Uncle Sammy, I'm afraid," Stoker used to mur-mur happily to himself as he stored his monies in the hotel safe each morning.

Out of sight, all over the convention, other actions were in progress to nudge the course of history.

The Governor of Louisiana, Ed Regis, and a few trusted henchmen were huddling over after-breakfast cigars and strong black coffee. "Ah tell you, fellas, it was un-canny, un-canny." Those present listened to the gov-ernor with the popeyed attention those who have jobs to dispense are able to command. "It was just like some-thin' a-crawlin' up out of the dark and nippin' at ya. Ah was sittin' there at the fights, watchin' a couple of pre-liminaries before the main bout, when Ah heard some-one say, 'In this corner—Dangle.'

" 'Did he say Dangle?' Ah asks Breck." Here the admir-ing glances shifted to Breck, who had been with the great man at such an instant. After a pause to slosh a little coffee around in his mouth, the governor contin-ued, "Breck, he looks at his program and says, 'By God, it is Dangle,' Breck says. So Ah says to Breck, 'Dangle's my boah.' 'He's mine too,' says Breck, because you know we wuz both strong Dangle men. Ah gives Breck a twenty and takes a twenty of his'n, and Ah tells him to go out and get us a little of the Kid—what wuz his name? Well, it don't matter. Ah tell him to go out and get a little of the Kid's money.

"He done just that. This guy Dangle looks good in

the first round, see. He's got a nice left—clean, see. Ah
see he's using the laces a bit in the clinches, and Ah
thinks to mahself, 'Here's where a little more of the
Northern money comes down to God's own state.'
Dangle's lookin' good in the second, too—real good.

"The gong goes for the third, see. Ah turns to Breck
and says, 'This is where Dangle finishes him off.' Then
bammo! The Kid lands a right and Dangle goes down,
glassy-eyed. When Ah seed them knees buckle slow"—
Dangle was nothing if not an artistic fight thrower—"Ah
figure it's all over. This Dangle, he's got a glass jaw.
Money—good-by." The governor paused and looked at
his dead cigar. Breck quickly leaned forward and lit it.

"Then Ah really get to thinking—maybe this is a sign.
All my life Ah been lucky cuz Ah follows mah stars. Mah
Mammy tole me, 'The day you see three 'gators chasing each other in a circle—that's your lucky year.' Ah
seen three 'gators chasing each other the week I filed for
governor. And you know who's the governor of the
greatest state in the Union today.

"Ah got a heap of change riding on that guy Dangle
that wants to run for President. Ah figure this here is a
sign that he got a glass jaw too. So I'm switchin'. And
Ah plans for all Louisiana to switch at our caucus this
afternoon. So pass the word and tell everybody to be on
time. Ah means this to be a legal caucus, and Ah wants
to be out at the dog track for the third race."

Late that evening, in a deserted hotel back corridor,
the chairman of the Oklahoma delegation, Lem Pitz,
and the Lieutenant Governor of Oklahoma were in earnest but absolutely motionless conversation. "Three for
you and three for me. You bring in the eastern delegates;

I'll bring in my western and take care of the governor."

"I thought you said we were going to get seven, Lemmie."

"We got six and hotel rooms, that's seven. All we could get from Dangle was five. Period."

"Okay."

An envelope came out of the chairman's inside pocket. "Here's your three. Now for God's sake don't begin spending it until we get home. We don't want anyone round here getting wise."

"What kind of a tenderfoot you think I am? Say, what we going to do about the senator? He keeps on talking to the press all the time and telling them Oklahoma will be for Dangle."

"The hell with him! He knows the press because he and they are buddy-buddy in Washington. Let him tell his Washington pals what he wants. We got the votes to take 'em in the state."

"Okay. You sure this Microvac is going to win?"

"Sure. You ever hear of anybody putting out seven thousand dollars that wasn't sure?"

"I thought you said we only got six."

The chairman, while not bright, was at least shifty. "Well, I was counting ours and the governor's rooms as another thousand."

"All right, when do we caucus?"

"Let's caucus late tomorrow afternoon. No point in giving Dangle's boys too much time to put the heat on us."

The great state of Oklahoma was going to be with Microvac all the way. So was the great state of Kansas, and a sizable hunk of the great state of Washington.

The convention floor at the Arena was an immovable
jam of yelling people. The moment of public truth approached. The last nominating speech had just ended,
and the delegates were working themselves into the
traditional frenzy before voting. Key floor command-
ers, surrounded by loyal cohorts to keep the unwanted
from overhearing, whispered instructions and reports
into short-wave radios. Demonstrating claques collided
with one another and with police trying to clear the
aisles. Beautiful girls, hired to parade the claims of various factions, were crushed by masses of delegates scurry-
ing, conferring, seeking their places. Above the crowd
waved banners bearing the devices of would-be cham-
pions. Through it all lunged reporters with microphones
and pencils, trying to catch the inflection or whisper that
would make them first with history. Everyone was rush-
ing, shouting, and plotting, while the heavy stamp of the
Chairman's gavel tried to bring order from the riot.

Dick Dolan gazed down at the packed confusion from
the press stand, impressed despite his professional
aplomb. You never could be absolutely certain what
would happen when so many people got together
openly for a climax. For all their seeming political sang-
froid, the delegates were men and women. Isolated in
the crowd below, they knew nothing but their own un-
stable mood. Rumors of fantastic happenings sizzled
about the floor. The whole convention might be exploded by a sudden demonstration in the galleries, the
right word from some minor figure swirling around the
great, an impassioned speech by a volunteer, or the
switch of a handful of votes at some unguessed vital in-

stant. The explosion would change history. Dolan had
seen that happen once. His head twitched, remembering
the almost killing excitement of those moments.

But here the odds were well over a hundred to one
against the unforeseen happening. The invisible political
leaders directing affairs by short wave and courier from
their suites off the convention floor would remain firmly
in control. There would be moments of exciting confusion when nothing seemed certain, but after each of
these the blocks would continue voting in predictable
patterns. And in the end, as Dolan had written that
morning, the mass would declare for Microvac.

Microvac had an awful lot going for him: the crucial
California victory, Indiana solidly in camp, Louisiana
and Oklahoma switching, Texas backing the machine.
The Microvac coalition was hard to figure, but it was
certainly powerful. Even Dangle's most ardent supporters were obviously jittery. Dolan guessed he'd start up
to Microvac's Arena headquarters when the voting got
underway.

Meanwhile he let the feverish excitement of the convention continue to infect him. He listened to the confused sounds of cheering, watched the people surge back
and forth, noted the eddies about those of importance.
There was Senator George Benbum, the supposedly neutral assistant convention chairman, who was ardently
pro-Dangle, conferring with a key Dangle aide, undoubtedly plotting some switch of votes. Right below Dolan
several rather tough-looking cops led by a huge pear-
shaped police sergeant were manhandling a Dangle band
off the floor. A group of reporters were pressing in around
Baird Tillsman, hurling questions at him about Micro-

vac's vice-presidential preferences. There was a flurry in
one of the boxes alongside the hall as Mr. Francis
Matchelder, followed by an aide with a two-way radio,
took his seat. A group of pretty girls wearing Microvac
sashes were having their way cleared for them by another group of tough cops. Someone in the Microvac
forces sure knows how to pick them, Dolan thought.

In the brief hiatus before voting started, Microvac
moved through the three rooms of its Arena headquarters. The machine thought this would be a good time
to reassure its campaign workers. The outer room was
jammed with telephoning staff members and harassed
camp followers, sandwiched between clusters of desks,
phones, typewriters, a mimeograph machine, large stocks
of paper, a two-way radio station, and a small switchboard. Kay Hard was at the board. Microvac's photoelectric eyes, automatically checking the room, ranged
over her for a fraction of a second. Her lipstick color
brought a response from its memory circuits. The same
unusual color had been on Fellows' neck. Microvac rapidly processed its Kay Hard data. She seemed the solution to the Fellows problem. The two tubes dealing
with current political strategy moved to other areas.

The machine rolled into the middle room—a conference room with a well-stocked bar—and greeted a few of
McGowan's friends. Then it retired to its own private
room, which had a large desk and two television sets.
The voting began.

As the vote went on, the phalanx, reinforced by
Waskey, had a harder and harder time holding back the
crowds outside the machine's suite. Inside, McGowan

was being deluged by important well-wishers frantically switching sides. Luke was supervising the mimeographing of Microvac's victory statement.

The private telephone on Microvac's desk rang. Conelli picked it up, listened, then held it toward Microvac. "Matchelder."

Mike waved in the direction of the TV sets to get them turned down.

"Microvac," the machine said flatly.

"Matchelder," came the dead voice on the other end of the phone. "I wanted to be among the first, perhaps the first from the other camp, to congratulate you on your magnificent triumph."

"Thank you."

"Naturally we must all work together for victory in November. I pledge to you my unswerving support. As a guaranty of that support, I want you to know that I am contributing, through various organizations, thirty thousand dollars to your campaign tomorrow morning."

"Thank you. I accept your pledge, and I welcome your opening contribution. Undoubtedly, as the campaign progresses, I will be hearing from you again." The machine hung up.

Just then there was a subdued roar from the turned-down TV sets. Conelli hiked up the volume. On the floor, delegates were cheering wildly. Microvac banners were waving up and down. Texas had just put Microvac over the top.

Well-wishers surged into the two outer offices, almost breaking down the plywood partition to Microvac's inner room. The phone on the machine's desk rang again.

The senior senator from Texas was coming up to claim his vice-presidential reward. Luke poked his head around the door to say that Whitey Bird was outside.

A day later, George Churpwell, Mayor of Detroit, was nominated for Vice President. There were loud cries of "deal" and shouts of vengeance from Texas, Pennsylvania, and Indiana. The leaders of all three swore publicly and privately that they would go fishing during the campaign.

"A solemn promise. I had your solemn promise!" Whitey Bird's entire form was tense with rage as he faced Microvac. "Doesn't a promise mean anything to you? You filthy machine!"

"It means as much to me as it does to you, Whitey, but the situation changed."

"And you"—Whitey turned on McGowan—"you, Mac, whom I have known for years—you could go along with this straight lie."

"Aw, Whitey—" began McGowan. It was no use. Whitey had his say for about twenty minutes and then was practically carried out by his aides, weak from anger and exhaustion.

"For a man who's meant to be a politician, he certainly doesn't understand the laws of politics," Microvac remarked to McGowan. "Don't you worry, Mac, we'll carry his state. Well, how does it feel, now that it's all over, to be managing a national candidate?" The machine put its arm warmly around McGowan, who, still without sleep, seemed practically unable to move.

"Good," said McGowan, numbly. "Good." He guessed he didn't feel anything because he was so tired.

CHAPTER EIGHT

OSBERT O'TOOLE, FAMED BRITISH HISTORIAN AND AMER-
ican correspondent for the London *Recorder*, surveyed
the United States political scene:

> WASHINGTON USA [O'Toole always added "USA" after
> "Washington" to locate that city exactly for the paper's
> older readers]:

> > "Breasting the mountains, cleaving the sea,
> > Brother, thy brother calls to thee."

So Catullus sounded the note to all brothers adown the
shrouded ages. Microvac, the electronic thinking machine, has breasted the mountain and gained the presidential nomination of the Demlican party, one of the
two great American parties. The question now is, who
is brother to the machine?

The answer of the Repicrats, the other great American political party, is, "No one"—followed by a loud
guffaw. Admiral Growley, just nominated as the Repicrats' candidate, is as well known in America as in
Europe. Americans have a historical tradition, which
they never admit to political consciousness, of electing
men on horseback in times of economic euphoria, a
tradition that dates back to their founding father,
George Washington.

Times are good in America, the fields fair and full,
the refrigerators loaded with tinned beer. The teeth of
the used-motor salesmen gleam aggressively, and the
national coffers bulge with the green fruits of unparal-

leled prosperity—dollars. The Repicrats are certain that
they, as the party in power, will benefit from this general well-being, and impartial statistics support this be-
lief.

Yet, for all this, a surprising number of people are
brother to the machine. Seven months ago Microvac
was an unknown calculator. Today he is running for
President. The machine has garnered this victory with
the slow, yet powerful persistence of the unfolding
primrose. Machine-minded Americans may yet be
minded by a machine. But for the present this does not
seem likely. Admiral Foster Growley, "the man who is
never wrong," appears destined to win over Mike
Microvac, "the machine who is always right."

Congressman Bates Hewball, "the sheep's friend," aggressively adjusted his first morning cigar. He was break-
fasting with that vital political group, the Sheriff's Hon-
orary Posse of Lonesome Forks. The cigar, Bates informed those around him as he stuffed in the last of
his eggs, fried potatoes, and pork chops, was made from
"All American tobacco! The man who puts somethin'
in his mouth some foreigner's spit on, don't think
much of his health or his country!" After a brief belch,
Bates rose to pass on the word.

"Now you all knows I didn't go to that convention
pledged to no candidate. Not bein' pledged gives more
chance to maneuver, see. When I got there I looked the
political situation over, and that ain't all I looked over.
They got some mighty fine fillies waggin' their watses
around that city of Chicago, yes sir! If any of you ever
go on a posse ride down there, leave the women and
children to home. That's real man's country!" The
members of the Sheriff's Posse rolled their muscular

paunches in a series of guffaws. Old Hewball—he sure was a rarin', tearin' ripsnorter!

"When I seed what was goin' on I went right in and done a little Western horse-tradin'. Some of them big Eastern money boys thought they was pretty big wheeler-dealers, but old Bates Hewball got the big pile of chips for this here state. Listen to this. Microvac is comin' here to make a speech on how our state needs more federal money, better irrigation, more power, and more free land for grazin' sheep." Bates's roaring voice paused to let the vision of federal dollars fluttering down over the land like soft snow sink into the avaricious minds of his listeners. "Microvac is comin' here into this state at the invitation of Bates Hewball, a man in his corner all the way. And remember a vote for Microvac and me means more dollars for our blessed state."

In the plush privacy of the East Side Club, a mansion-away-from-mansion for the rich, Matchelder, his hooded eyes flickering behind expensive cigar smoke, gave a business crony his version of the world. "It is undeniably true—undeniably true and public knowledge—that I went to the convention firmly committed to Bryant Dangle. I have, frankly, known Bryant all my life. To use an expression I will ask you to forget the instant I have used it, Bryant is one of us. But politics, like the law, deals with reality.

"Shortly after arriving at the convention I received certain private intelligence that convinced me the machine actually had a better chance of beating Admiral

Growley than Bryant did. Therefore, while out of personal loyalty I remained committed to Bryant, I was not too unhappy or surprised when the convention swung the other way. I called Mike early on the final day and explained the situation. Mike realized just the way the land lay and appreciated my loyalty to Bryant. After the convention he accepted me enthusiastically into the fold." Matchelder paused and sucked in his lips as if savoring the juice of some lush plum of political office dribbling down his jowls.

"I wonder if you, or your firm—I know your politics are different from mine—would consider making, shall we say, a small investment in democracy. If you would, I would be glad to apprise Microvac personally of your generosity."

Admiral Foster Growley prided himself that his Repicrat headquarters was a "tight ship." Even the babies he kissed were inspected before he handled them— this had rather thrown Waskey off stride. Now his cold eye ranged over his campaign staff during the regular morning briefing. Two aides were demonstrating the difference between his position on civil rights and Microvac's. The Admiral's past speeches on the subject had been culled. Just where he stood was being explained to him. A series of forceful *hums* exploded out of Growley's flaring nostrils like the exhaust of a starting jet. Suddenly Growley took off with the ill-concealed impatience of one who feels his time wasted by nincompoops.

"Goddamn it! Don't tell me where I stand on civil

rights. I know where I stand. I've always been for all real Americans. If they are good enough to die equally, they're good enough to live equally. Now this machine, Microvac—I know where he stands, too. He doesn't stand with me. No siree! If he stood with me he wouldn't be running against me. This machine isn't for people. He's for himself and the selfish men around him.

"You know why the machine can't be for people?" Admiral Growley continued, his sunlamp-tanned face flushing with the intensity of his own brilliance. "The machine can't be for people because he has no mother! You can't trust something that doesn't have a mother. I have a mother." The admiral's aides and political advisers stared in amazement at Growley's ability to cut to the quick of a problem. Here they were, frantically trying to hang Microvac on the machine's nonexistent record. Growley had seized upon a basic issue. And those bright newspapermen continually went around saying the admiral didn't know anything about politics!

"Now, let's get down to basics." Growley shot out of his chair and began to move around the room. "That's what I always did in the Navy. I've had—I think I may safely say so—I've had some little experience in getting down to basics."

"Yes, sir. You have, sir." The staff's chorused reply crackled through the room.

"How fast can you steam? That's what I used to ask my Navy staff when they came up with some fancy-type study. Answering a tough question like that separates the men from the boys."

"It certainly does, sir," the staff chorused, quickly divining that only boys doubted admirals.

"Last night as I was going to bed I asked myself a few basic questions about our opponent. Now, I don't mind having an opponent. They are part of the American system; if you read your history you'll see that. Where, I asked myself, did Microvac learn what was good? How to pray? The meaning of discipline?" Growley flung himself back in his swivel chair, set his constantly gesticulating hands on his knees, and shot his body forward so that his massive chin seemed a concentrated battering ram of force. "Where did we all learn this? From our dear mothers. Now Microvac never had a mother and therefore never learned about God, right and wrong. In my next broadcast—and it should be soon, we've got to steam—I intend to follow the course of duty on this issue."

"What about the orphan vote?" questioned an alert young aide.

"We can't be thinking about the orphan vote at a time like this, young man," replied Growley, tilting his head to one side and thrusting out his lips. "This is a question of principle. Besides, there are very few orphans. I guess you speech-writing chaps can take it from there."

Take it from there they did, through twelve highly polished drafts. Each one got a little closer to calling Microvac an atheistic mechanical bastard without actually saying so. A tintype view of Admiral Growley's happy home life and boyhood Christmases was contrasted with the plight of those unfortunates who drifted motherless about the world. After this contrast, Growley's speech moved on quickly to discuss the farm problem. The admiral still felt that he was above politics and saw no reason to knee Microvac when he had the machine on the mat, godless and motherless.

Growley's running mate, Samuel Shoemaker— "Shifty Sam Shoemaker," to his opposition—had a rather callused knee. "I ask you," said Sam, following up Admiral Growley's attack a few nights later, "I ask all you good people who have let me come into your home through television this evening: Can a machine who has never known the steadying influence of home, God, and mother be entrusted with your vote? Can you expect honest government from something that has had no mother?" Some of the more cynical viewers expected Sam to claim he had three mothers. However, he stopped short of this, merely having his Mom come on and embrace him while an unseen orchestra struck up "Home, Sweet Home."

The ranks of Microvac's national headquarters in New York City reeled beneath the implications of being successfully labeled Godless and motherless. Luke and McGowan held a hurried conference with Microvac to devise a counterattack. They found the machine unperturbed.

"I've seen this coming for some time."

"Why didn't you tell us then, Microvac, sir?" Luke gasped. "We could have made certain preparations."

"There were four obvious lines of attack against me: I had no mother; I am Godless; I have charged my batteries with public power; I don't bathe. I knew I would have to face some of these issues. Now here is the speech I intend to deliver next week before the All Faith Committee. See if you think it answers Growley."

The All Faith Committee turned out to be an ideal TV audience. It was quiet, proper, and important enough to sustain the illusion that Microvac was making a speech rather than giving a television performance. The religious nature of the gathering cast an air of sanctity and seriousness over what was said. Even the omnipresent press photographers had been barred. Their leader had approached the bishop chairing the conference and suggested, "Hey, Bish, I hope you're goin' to get some broads up in the front row this year to sex up them prayers. Christ! It was dead here last year!" The bishop, a new bishop who hadn't dealt with the press before, strangely took offense.

The key portion of Microvac's speech was the peroration. The machine had carefully built up to this emotional moment with a moving account of America's religious history. Then came the clincher.

"The opposition has intimated that I am Godless. Is there no known depth to which they will not sink? How could I, a humble machine that knows all the answers, be Godless? For I know where I get my juice. Do I run on my own current? Do I generate my own power? Do I motivate myself? No. Someone far greater than I put the water in the rivers to make the power to give me life. I know Whose master hand gave me the joy of being alive. I know I get my joy juice from God. Not for one single instant do I ever forget from whence cometh my joy juice."

The members of the All Faith Religious Committee

rose to their feet to give the machine burst after burst of prolonged applause. The next day the Committee voted to adopt a national prayer slogan suggested by Microvac:

> Is your Joy Juice on today?
> If not, brother, start to pray.

Microvac had struck an all-American religious gong. Clergymen vied with each other in extolling Microvac as the example of true religious life. Several papers that had been editorially against the machine changed over, citing Microvac's religious virtues. Complaints that the machine had not adequately defined its "joy juice" were dismissed as anti-God and therefore un-American.

After that, on Sundays, when Microvac paraded to church, there were vast crowds on hand to see the machine enter and emerge. On leaving, Microvac always commented knowingly on the sermon and quoted a few appropriate texts from the Bible. The machine never bothered to record permanently anything said in church. But it did record the answers it made on leaving. In this way Microvac's attitude toward religion was as oriented toward political victory as was everything else.

"Mike, you really did it," said McGowan to the machine a few days later, when he had had time to assess the national reaction. "Old Growley is going to have to get up awfully early on a Sunday morning to get closer to God than you."

"We're all right in the press," said Luke. "A great job."

"All right is the key word," said Microvac. "We've stopped that attack, but we aren't any better off—

probably a little worse off. Some doubt always remains after a denial. Being merely all right does not make me feel any too well. We have to get moving."

There it was again, thought McGowan, the machine's born understanding of politics. At the word "born" he checked himself. Since Microvac had no mother, did it have "born understanding"? McGowan winced.

A few days later Microvac shoved the throttle to the flame wall on its own campaign. The machine's basic strategy was continuous travel. Moving rapidly across the country, it multiplied the expenses of the reporters and cameramen chasing it. Since Microvac stories cost so much, editors assumed they must be excellent. They gave the traveling Microvac major play in the press and choice television time. Also, by traveling, the machine was able to demonstrate its extraordinary local knowledge. Millions of voters, experiencing Microvac's tireless energy and personal touch at first hand, became convinced that Microvac cared more for them than Growley did.

The invasion of Missouri, home state of the opposition vice-presidential candidate, "Saluting Samuel Shoemaker, America's red, white, and blue hope for peace," was a typical Microvac operation. The machine flew from its New York headquarters to St. Louis one morning, then that night went on to Seattle, Washington. It had breakfast next morning in Seattle and did a little campaigning in the suburbs, then took off for Kansas City by way of Minneapolis, to hit Missouri again. All across the land experts spoke of the unprecedented vigor and vitality of Microvac's campaign.

Each trip was minutely scheduled to enable Microvac to shake the last ounce of political value from every minute of local time. At first Microvac did most of the scheduling itself, sending advance men into the area a few days before with detailed instructions. But as the pace grew faster and Microvac was almost constantly in flight, McGowan assumed almost all the important job of scheduling. Microvac could not both direct its campaign and campaign itself; the job was not too complex, but too time-consuming.

Microvac realized that McGowan, while performing highly adequately, couldn't analyze all the factors going into a perfect traveling day. That job was beyond human capability. The machine was forced to spend long hours with McGowan between trips, rearranging future scheduling details.

A few hours before taking off on an eight-day, fourteen-state campaign swing in early October, Microvac and McGowan were alone in the machine's suite. The two had just finished a final look at the trip plans. Microvac had made a series of detailed changes and asked a number of pertinent questions McGowan hadn't been able to answer.

"I could help you more, Mike," said McGowan as he got heavily to his feet to put the changes into effect, "if I just had a quarter of your brain and didn't need sleep. Maybe what you need is another machine."

Microvac looked at McGowan closely. The machine had considered bringing Repcal I secretly to New York to handle trip-planning details. However, Microvac had decided that McGowan would have violent objections, even though to outsiders he would still appear to be running things. "There are some things machines can't do." Microvac was noncommital.

"Yes, blow up balloons. Remember that day in Ohio?" Mac paused, allowing himself a few moments of relaxation in thinking of the past. "I'm just as glad there's only you, Mike. I've been an assistant campaign manager before. It's unpleasant. Say, this campaign has sure put you behind schedule with that second machine."

"That second machine may never get made," said Microvac with pensive warmth. It had been right; bringing in another machine was impossible. "I just don't know if I ever will get round to it."

"Well, Mike, once you get to the White House, anything you do will be okay with me."

"Thanks, Mac." The two walked toward the corridor door, arm in arm. "When I get to the White House, anything you do is okay with me, too."

Shortly after McGowan left, there was a diffident knock at the machine's door. The boyish face of Professor Fellows poked itself inside. Fellows was visibly agitated. His floppy blond forelock drooped about his eyes more than usual. His disjointed legs were almost individually propelled. Fellows realized he appeared this way. He was about to lie to Microvac. He was certain Microvac had made some changes in himself, and he had no idea what qualities the machine now possessed. Maybe Microvac contained a lie-detector.

"Microvac," said Fellows, advancing spasmodically but cautiously into the room, "I'm afraid I won't be able to make this trip. I have a fever of a hundred and three, and the doctor says I'm coming down with a bad case of the grippe. I've explained to Conelli how to change the battery packs, and I can't see any cause for trouble. I'm very sorry."

Fellows jiggled nervously from one leg to the other as Microvac, expressing its condolences, rolled over and laid its hand on Fellows' brow. The professor wondered how much the sensitized electronic plates on the machine's hands could feel. "Yes, you are ill. You are running a fever of a hundred and three point two. You had better get to bed."

"Yes, I guess so," the scientist agreed with a falsetto wheeze and began to back from the room.

"After all," Microvac called after him, "we've got to get you safely through this campaign so that you can see more of Kay Hard." The machine believed in being friendly with its staff. Besides, the knowledge of how much it knew kept them working harder.

Fellows' feet tangled with each other. Leaving Microvac's door open, he bolted. His first reaction was that Microvac could read minds. He realized that was wrong. If Microvac had read his mind, it would have known he was not sick but had merely drugged himself with trinitrophenol to raise his temperature. Besides, he had seen Microvac make big mistakes with people. The machine must have discovered some other way.

The machine's knowledge made no difference. He would still go down to East Virginia as soon as Microvac left. He had to see Kay. They hadn't met since Chicago, and the more he campaigned the more he missed her. They had been telephoning back and forth. Kay's in-laws-to-be were going away for three days, starting tomorrow. He and Kay were to meet in a motel a safe distance from the university. At least, Fellows thought they would meet. He couldn't be sure.

"I'll get there first, Proffy, and take care of things," Kay had said. "Even if you were married, you wouldn't look legal. As a matter of fact, I just may not be there. This has got to stop."

"Oh, Kay!" he had begged.

"It won't hurt you to make the trip anyway. Travel is broadening."

Kay turned up. Fellows, bursting to tell her what Microvac had said, kept quiet. Kay changed so fast. One moment everything was fine; then she'd start badgering him about the future; next she'd be irritated at herself and mad at him for not understanding. He didn't want to say anything that might drive her away.

Finally, late the second afternoon, with just one night left, his news came out. Kay was after him for being even more jumpy than usual.

"Well, I am nervous," Fellows admitted, patting her with the feigned assurance of a small boy stroking a puppy he thinks might bite. "Microvac knows about us."

She sat up and turned on him. "Proffy, you fool! You told him."

"No, no, I didn't. Microvac just popped it out at me, after I told him I was sick."

"And you jumped all over the place and said, 'Yes, sir, yes, sir, yes, sir.' "

"I didn't say anything. No. I don't know how he knew."

"Probably he saw you staring at me or something in Chicago, and guessed. You're horrible at hiding things."

"I know, but you can't tell. There's parts of Microvac you just can't tell about. Take the first night Microvac went bowling. He went out bowling at ten, when I was coming over the roof to see you. Yet I heard what sounded like him in the laboratory. It could have been just some test relay he'd set up, but there's things like that that just bother me—though I've been too busy to bother much."

"Why didn't you look?"

"You can't look. I tried a few nights later. The lab's all locked up when Mike's out—venetian blinds over the windows. There's just a little space at the top. You can't see anything but ceiling."

"If I was a man I'd find out. Mike found out about us. You may like the machine, you helped with parts of him, but he's—well he's not—I don't like him."

"That's irrational."

"You're just scared."

"Scared of what?" Fellows was sullen.

"Scared to take a peak at your dear machine's laboratory. If you wanted, you could figure out a little thing like that. Chop a hole in the roof, or something."

"The roof is concrete."

Kay curled up like an annoyed hedgehog and turned away from him.

In the end, Fellows drove to a five-and-ten and bought himself a cheap fishing rod, some pocket mirrors, and a box of large paper clips.

Shortly after two that morning Fellows parked his car in a small lane close to the laboratory. Once he had returned with the equipment and plan, Kay had been wonderful. He had just dropped her off near her house. Now, as he got out, he noticed that the ground was soaking from a recent rain. He should be wearing rubbers. Then the incongruity of worrying about catching cold made him even more frightened.

He was frightened. He was about to spy on Microvac. He had no idea what the machine did to people who spied, but he had seen enough of its calculated efficiency to have no intention of finding out.

His plan called for climbing the laboratory rainspout, using his old route to Kay in reverse. The winter-stiff rhododendron leaves around the building made an alarming rattle as he pushed through. In front was his friendly gutterspout, metallically cold. He paused, then began pulling himself up from support to support. All around him he could hear noises; he hoped they were just ordinary night sounds magnified by his intense listening. He pulled himself over the roof's edge. There was no one there.

He began to make his way over the flat concrete. The little pebbles beneath his feet made a terrible scuttling sound. He didn't remember making so much noise when he was going to see Kay. He lay down and wormed his way to the roof's edge approximately over Microvac's laboratory window. He took the fishing-rod parts out of his pocket and joined them. On the rod's end he clipped a mirror. He thrust the crude periscope over the edge and found himself a little to the right of the windows. Again there was a brief period of squirming. Fellows wondered what the wet roof surface was doing to his clothes. Fortunately, it didn't matter; he had another suit in the car. Once more he thrust the periscope forward.

Now, by tilting the rod upward, he could peer inside Microvac's laboratory. At first his slight shiver and the smallness of the mirror made it hard to recognize what he saw. Finally, by adjusting the mirror, he made out quite a bit of the lower part of the laboratory.

Suddenly he saw something move along the lab floor. He was looking at another set of tracks just like Microvac's. As he watched, the first set was followed by a second, then a third. Tilting the rod to get a view of what was fastened to the tracks, Fellows thought for an instant that he was looking at Microvac. Then he realized that he was looking at three Microvacs—or at three machines that appeared exactly like Microvac. The three machines rolled over to a workbench running along the side of the laboratory. There they began to work with precise, rapid movements. Fellows withdrew the rod. He was shaking so he couldn't get it apart.

Microvac had already completed not just one machine, but several. Perhaps even now those machines below were building more. He felt sudden panic and wrenched the rod apart. If Microvac wanted to hide this process, there was a reason. Microvac did everything for reasons. To the machine he would be more than a spy. He would be a traitor. Fellows went down the drainpipe so fast he cut his hands on the iron wall fastenings.

Two evenings later Fellows entered McGowan's office. Like everyone else in the organization with a problem, he had gone to the obvious place. McGowan existed to solve problems.

Fellows had tried to see McGowan immediately after getting back from East Virginia. But a day and a half had gone by before he could fight his way past the confusion in the outer offices and see Mac alone.

"Hi, Doc," said McGowan when Fellows finally managed to slip in between two delegations. "Good to see you. You know, you're the one guy in this organization that practically never bothers me." McGowan's greeting was genuinely warm. His liking for Fellows had grown during the campaign. The doc was even good with visiting firemen when they blundered into him—a fine Joe.

"You're hard to get to see, Mac. It took me a day and a half."

"What?" McGowan exploded. "You're on the list of people who are to get in to me any time." He pulled out one of his innumerable slips of paper and made a note. "What's on your mind? No serious beef, I hope."

"Beef? No, not a serious beef," said Fellows, abandoning his carefully rehearsed speech under McGowan's easy informality. "Just that we've got a definite problem."

"We? Those are the kind I don't like. Sit down," said McGowan, rising himself. "What's the pitch?"

"It's about Microvac."

McGowan's sharp intake of breath practically sucked the papers off his desk. "Not something wrong with the mechanism? A loose circuit? A jammed tube?"

"No," said Fellows slowly, watching the tips of his interlaced fingers turn red and then white under the pressure he was putting on them. "No, it's more complex than that. When we built into Microvac the ability to make other machines like himself, we decided— we being the scientists in the Defense Department and

East Virginia—we decided we would have Microvac make only one machine. These advanced calculators can be a little bit tricky to handle. We didn't want to start what we used to call the 'Sorcerer's Apprentice reaction' of machines building machines. After all, there is a limit to this machine business." Fellows didn't know why he added the last sentence, but it popped out with a rather high-voltage crackle. He realized with a start that he must be masking more latent hostility toward Microvac than he realized.

"You're damn right there's a limit. I don't mind telling you, Doc, I was relieved the other day when Microvac told me he wasn't making any more."

"Well, he has made more." Fellows' voice was low and slow. "Or, to be accurate, he has both made more himself and probably caused other machines made by him to make more. I went down to the university— Don't tell anybody, particularly Microvac. You won't tell anybody?"

"Don't worry; half of politics is keeping secrets."

"Well, I went down to East Virginia University two days ago to see some friends, when I got over being sick. I know the place pretty well, and I just happened to get a look into Microvac's laboratory—scientific curiosity. You know it's always closed. I couldn't look for long, a minute to a minute and a half, but in that time I saw three machines, each of which—of whom—of which— It doesn't matter. They all looked enough like Microvac to be Microvac himself."

"Did they move?"

"They were working."

"Damn it." McGowan paced the room rapidly,

blowing out his cheeks. "Why didn't Mike tell me he
was making more machines? I can understand him wanting to keep it quiet. More machines would ruin us with
the voters. This machine angle is tricky enough as it
is. But why not tell me? In fact he told me different."
Out of loyalty McGowan deliberately avoided the word
"lie."

"And me, and all the scientists. He fooled us all.
That's the point. Microvac has a reason. We should face
the machine and find out what that reason is."

"Yeah, we should," said McGowan, immersed in his
own thoughts.

"Just as soon as Microvac gets back from this trip
we should go in together and have it out."

McGowan looked closely at Fellows. "Look, Doc,
when I was younger I was always facing people and
having it out—and whipping them, too. Now I'm an old
guy and I'm getting fat and I shove little suppositories up
my tail to ease my piles. I don't face things so often any
more. Let's not get in some bind we can't get out of.
Let me bring this matter up to Microvac alone at the
right moment, and see what he has to say. There's no
point in two of us getting messed up in this thing.
If you're there, he'll guess you went to East Virginia.
I'm going to get involved in it sooner or later; I might
just as well take it from the beginning."

"All right. This isn't the sort of thing I'm used to."
Fellows had been hoping that McGowan would take
over. "If you feel you should do it alone, okay. But it
must be done."

"Right." McGowan turned toward him and smiled
reassuringly. "I'll find out." As he walked to the door,

his arm around Fellows, he was inwardly amused. He liked the doc. People told him Doc was one of the real comers in advanced physics. Yet Fellows wanted to ask Microvac why he was doing something the machine was trying to hide. No wonder poor scientists were always being suckered by Communists and people like that. You didn't ask people why they were hiding things. You figured it out.

This one was easy. Microvac was making more machines because Mike thought machines helped him more than humans did. Machines could do everything that mattered, while people fronted for them. Mike was keeping the new machines secret so human beings wouldn't know he thought them bums until after the election. But there was no need to bother young Doc with such problems. Doc was so nervous he'd mess up any approach to Microvac.

Above all, the machine had lied to him, its manager, the unpardonable political sin. You could do anything you wanted to the enemy. They did it to you. You might make an end run around friends because you didn't want to hurt their feelings. You might keep quiet about something. But you didn't lie to your own guys. Yet with so little time before the election, should he talk to Microvac?

As they reached the door, McGowan gripped Fellows firmly on the shoulder. "Don't worry, Doc, I'll take care of it." He had used the same expression, gesture, and tone to thousands on thousands of troubled voters. There was magic in the effect. "And Doc, one more thing. This whole business has got to be kept to ourselves. It's murder politically."

"I wasn't going to tell anybody but you."

"Good." McGowan went back to his desk, feeling as limp and empty as the cigarette pack he had been crumpling in his pocket. The thought that, whatever happened, he should be okay, was hardly consolation.

CHAPTER NINE

THE TWO JET TRANSPORTS CARRYING MICROVAC, THE MA-chine's staff, and the press following them were whining at four hundred knots through the predawn blackness between Savannah, Georgia, and Fort Wayne, Indiana. In the past six days Microvac had been energetic and warm in twelve states. This pace—inhuman or super-human, depending on the commentator's politics—had reduced the machine's staff and the reporters to numb exhaustion. Microvac rolled on, shaking hands, soothing babies, making friends, settling disputes, jazzing up local organizations, and giving television speeches to vast na-tional audiences swollen by news of the machine's alive campaign.

The Fort Wayne airport toward which the planes were racing was still practically deserted. Three rotund middle-aged men, wearing Microvac hats, stared out over the concrete beginning to heat up in the morning sun. Part-time political workers, they had not been told when to arrive, so they had come early to miss no chance of being seen with the great. A state police car rolled up with Joe Waskey. Waskey was Microvac's advance man for Indiana, because Indiana, with its Whitey Bird prob-lem, was a tough state. Waskey was out of sorts. He had been up till four for the last five mornings, arguing with the Indiana organization. The detailed directives from Microvac's New York headquarters were tricky to execute. Making people do what they were told when they didn't want to or have to was difficult.

Irritably surveying the airport, Waskey noted that the manager had strung rope barriers everywhere. Waskey had told the manager not to do this three days ago. But he realized the manager was of the officious type who believe no one should talk to the great but themselves. The sound truck over which Microvac would address the airport crowds had arrived, with banners reading: "Art Randall's Sound Service—Best in the World." Waskey had ordered Microvac banners for that truck. Some fool must have paid Art Randall in advance.

Suddenly two flashes of weird green light lit the airport, followed by ear-splitting cracks. The Joy Wagon had arrived. Its neon-lighted sides were ablaze with the new slogan: "Join the Joy Wagon. Vote Microvac." There were now three Joy Wagons leap-frogging from stop to stop to parade with Microvac. This Joy Wagon had sprinted in from New Orleans, where it had led the Microvac rally day before yesterday. The Joy Wagon from Savannah, which Microvac had left at two that morning, was racing to Grand Rapids, Michigan, for tomorrow. The Florida Joy Wagon, in action yesterday afternoon, was tooling for New York to welcome the machine back to headquarters.

While Waskey was persuading the airport manager to take down the barriers, the faithful began to arrive. Local candidates for Congress and the state legislature breezed in, gripping one another's hands warmly to unlimber their vital palmar muscles. The inevitable Indians, without which no candidate can campaign west of the Hudson, took their places impassively on the concrete runway, resplendent in war bonnets. You sure can buy Indians cheap, thought Waskey. The white man fleeces them for years and pays them off with an occasional public handshake from a junketeering politician.

The state chairman and the lieutenant governor descended on him. They wanted one more man on the first truck. Microvac had substituted two flat-bed trucks and two buses for the long line of cars composing the traditional political motorcade. The machine believed that the old-time caravan created traffic jams, made motorists mad, and lost votes. The Microvac system whisked the same number of people through traffic with far less delay. Microvac rode on a small dais in the center of the first truck, surrounded by the most important officials. Behind this truck came the Joy Wagon, with arrows pointing at Microvac. The machine had observed that in most parades the crowd waved at the wrong person. After the Joy Wagon came the second truck with lesser officials. Finally, in the two buses, came really inferior officials, Microvac's staff, and the press.

Waskey explained patiently, as he had over and over again during the past five days, the careful balance of professional politicians, citizens' groups, Negroes, labor leaders, and big money that would ride in the first truck. He permitted the two officials to palaver with him long and earnestly to save face. The passes that let people on the first truck were in his brief case. He could afford to say no politely. Finally he was able to slip away to make certain that the trucks and buses were set to go. They were all okay except the crucial lead truck. It had only an eighth of a tank of gas.

"I don't know where I'm goin', or who I'm drivin', or nuttin'," said the driver. "Some other guy is meant to be drivin' this truck, see? Jesus! I'm still in bed when the flippin' phone rings and its the big boss—not just the boss, the big boss. He says to shake it and get this truck out here. And, buddy, when the big boss says, 'Shake,' you shake. I hear I'm drivin' a ball team."

"You got a union card?"

"You ever try hustlin' a truck in this state without one?"

"Okay. Now look, you're going to be carrying Mike Microvac, see? Mike Microvac, the next President of the United States."

"No bull? That machine who knows everythin'? He's goin' to be the next President? It's been fixed, huh? Good, I'm for him myself. I'm glad the fix is in. I was worried about that admiral guy."

"Now look," Waskey spoke slowly, impressing each word on the driver. "I'm Microvac's manager. I'm running this convoy. Don't let anybody else tell you anything. I'm going to see the airport manager and have him gas you up. Then all you have to do all day is follow that white police car in front of you. It's the only white police car in the parade. And use the john before we get going. We'll be driving all day."

"And I ain't had my coffee. Okay."

Nothing, thought Waskey glumly, gets done in politics unless you do it yourself. Rechecking the airport, he noticed with alarm that one of the Indians was carry-

ing an extra war bonnet. He headed rapidly across the
runway toward the man.

"Morning, Chief. What's this bonnet?"

"For Microvac."

"I thought we agreed two days ago Microvac was to
get a war drum."

"Drum not worthy of such great leader. I think bonnet better. Last six guys I've met all got bonnets."

With all my other troubles, thought Waskey, I should
find an Indian who thinks. "Look, Chief, Microvac, he
machine. Here picture Microvac." He reached hastily
into his pocket and pulled out a newspaper clipping of
himself and the machine at Chicago, which he carried
to show friends. "See, Microvac got no head. All world
know machine got no head. You give bonnet to machine that got no head, you look silly to whole world,
Chief. All these people here say, 'Dumb Indian. Indian
doesn't know machine has no head.' I no want that,
Chief. Microvac no want that. He loves Indians, especially descendants of Snow-in-the-Face, like yourself.
You give him drum as planned. Okay?"

"Okay. But drum not here. Drum back in motel."

The two men looked at each other briefly with the
dejection born of sudden and unexpected defeat.
"What's that blue bead bracelet you're wearin' there,
Chief?"

"Just bracelet."

"You give that to Microvac?"

"Why?"

"Microvac would like it. The machine has arms.
Here's twenty for the bracelet and another twenty for
the bonnet. Give me that bonnet. I'll take care of that.

Now look, this bracelet is the victory bracelet of the thunderbird. You get that? If reporters ask—victory bracelet of the thunderbird. Very important gift. Okay?"

"Okay. Comes from five-and-ten."

Waskey had already passed on. He noticed that Senator Jim Freeman had arrived, and he pushed toward him, trying to filter his way through the layers of sanitation inspectors, water commissioners, county sheriffs, judges, and other political substrata now thronging the airport. A loud buzzing started up from his inside coat pocket. Microvac's plane was in range of the field, and his miniature short-wave radio was responding to the plane's call. Waskey pushed the Indian bonnet at a small child. "Here, kid, have a twenty-buck bonnet. Whaddya mean, what should you do with it? Whaddya think you should do with it? Now run along before I do it for you."

He pulled the tiny radio set out and spoke to the plane. Conelli was on the other end. Waskey reported no surprises.

"We got one thing here." Conelli's voice was fuzzy but audible. "Darlene Lord is traveling with us. She won't make the motorcade, but she will get off the plane for pictures. Tell the local photographers and TV men. The press plane knows. We're going to give the press a few minutes to set up before we land. And Darlene wants a hotel suite in Indianapolis. Can you take care of that?"

"She won't make the motorcade, but will get off the plane for pictures and needs a hotel suite for tonight in Indianapolis. Right?"

"Right. And I'd like a telegraph agent. Out."

Waskey was already moving at top speed toward Senator James Freeman.

"Hi, Joe," the senator greeted him warmly. "How does it look?"

By the time Waskey had briefed the senator, sent the senator's secretary off to arrange for Darlene's hotel suite, and located a telegraph agent, the press plane was on the ground and the TV technicians were assaulting its belly, dragging out their heavy equipment. Microvac's plane, the two jet engines nearest the crowd cut, was taxiing across the field.

Microvac's plane rolled to a stop. The exit ramp was pushed across the shimmering concrete to the plane's door. The door swung open, and the crowd peered hopefully into the darkness inside. Waskey, watching with everybody else, felt a momentary pang that he was not inside. On the plane with the candidate—that was the place to make yourself felt, meet visiting dignitaries, make political time. Who cared about the advance man?

Conelli was first off the plane. He bounced down the ramp, making sure that it was secure in an unostentatious way. Then a few other aides pressed their way out, carrying brief cases bulging with money-raising plans, speech drafts, lists of union officials and political contacts, plane-stowage charts. Then there was a pause. Mike's energy and memory certainly enabled him to travel with an awfully small staff, thought Waskey. But where was Fellows? The doc with his small emergency repair kit was usually the last man off the plane before Microvac. Then he remembered that the doc was sick and wasn't making the trip.

The black doorway of the plane yawned, empty and dark. The crowd pressed forward. Microvac let them wait for a few seconds. Then the machine's squat bulk rolled through the door. The sunlight glinted dully on its gunmetal surfaces. As always, there was a slight hesitation in the crowd. They were all prepared for Microvac, yet the instant of surprise at seeing a machine remained. Microvac raised its hands confidently above its head. A roar of "We want Mike" broke out. Mike Microvac had arrived in another town.

Microvac rolled down the ramp, handshake, memory, and voice all working to project an aura of broad friendliness. The crowd surged in around the machine, handshakers, politicians, photographers, reporters, police, mechanics, all caught up in the infectious electrification of being near the great. The machine greeted the local dignitaries in the correct pecking order, then began shaking hands generally. The envious in the rear pushed forward. Those in front held back so as not to seem overanxious. Shrill cries of "I shook hands with him; really, I'm never going to wash this hand" went up from middle-aged ladies who would have punished their daughters for less fuss over a crooner. Around the fringes the machine's staff made contact with key local officials.

Then for an instant the whole hive of activity ceased. Darlene Lord was coming down the plane's ramp. Not even the presidential candidate of one of America's two great political parties, the first machine ever to run for public office, could compete with that. Darlene seemed to flow toward the ground in a fascinating series of clockwise and counterclockwise glides and falls. A perfect campaign adjunct, thought Microvac.

The high-school band once again proved America a nation of individuals by striking up, almost simultaneously, several arrangements of "The Star-Spangled Banner." As the last notes died into the hangars around the airport, Microvac and Darlene mounted a small speakers' platform. The machine exhorted the faithful, thanked all the local dignitaries for being present, commented on the excellent air of Indiana, and introduced Darlene Lord. Darlene said a few brief words about how Microvac was going to revitalize the home.

Waskey signaled to the band, which struck up "Onward, Christian Soldiers," Microvac's favorite hymn. "Everyone in their places! We're moving out," he yelled.

Microvac said good-by to Darlene with an affectionate squeeze of the hand. Politicians leaped for seats closest to Microvac on the truck. Reporters closed their notebooks. TV cameramen yanked desperately at their cables. The police cleared a path for Microvac to reach its place on the lead truck. The state police, the county police, the town police, the airport police, and the state commissioner of safety held a final argument on precedence at the front of the column. Then sirens on the motorcycles and squad cars cut on, the Joy Wagon launched two thunderbolts into the air, the trucks' wheels began to move. Anguished cries of "Where's Bill? Where's Charlie? Where's Frank?" went up. The crowd cheered. The state tour had begun.

The caravan rolled down the highway. On both trucks local politicians elbowed one another for choice places by the rail. There were no broken bones, but a newcomer on the second truck made the mistake of waving to a voter with both hands. Seeing him violate the political

rule, "One hand for the voter, the other for yourself,"
the old-timers at his sides sank their elbows into his
midriff. He staggered back while they quickly expanded
along the rail.

On the lead truck, Microvac surveyed the country-
side. A soft fall day drowsed magnificently across the
land. The machine sampled the median height of five
thousand cornstalks selected at random, noted that the
hourly temperature was 2.5 degrees above the normative
average, analyzed the precise shade of green on suburban
lawns, and classified the percentage of russet leaves still
remaining on the maples. A good day to comment on
the fine Indiana weather, Microvac decided.

Sirens screaming, the cavalcade hit the first town. The
town police were out in force—all nine of them—their
mauve dress-uniform pants drawn painfully together
over the folds of bulging bellies. In the center of town,
before the courthouse, the frenzied faithful filled the
square with cheers, and a high-school band blared
forth. A small knot of local officials was gathered around
the base of the tiny flag-draped grandstand, whose top
overflowed with collapsible chairs rented from a local
undertaking parlor. As Microvac's truck halted, the
welcoming committee started toward it with the confused surge of a wave breaking against a fast tide.

Everyone in town felt important as the machine
rolled onto the grandstand. Even Repicrats felt that
they had made holding the town so vital to the Demlicans that Microvac had to stop there. The mayor moved
to the microphone. The mayor introduced the assemblyman. The assemblyman introduced Senator Freeman.
Senator Freeman introduced the state senator. The state

senator introduced the national committeewoman. The national committeewoman introduced the state committeeman. The state committeeman introduced the national committeeman. The national committeeman introduced the state committeewoman. The state committeewoman introduced the local candidate for Congress. And the local candidate for Congress then introduced "The next President of the United States, Mike Microvac."

By then the crowd had heard the phrase "great American, great Indianan, great Demlican, and great public servant" eleven times. Their roar on greeting Microvac was partly one of relief.

Microvac had nothing of importance to say. This was deliberate. The big afternoon news story across the land would be Darlene Lord and her appeal for votes at the airport. A new story would be wasted on top of that. Worse, it might get in the way of tomorrow's news, which the machine's evening television speech would make. The reporters knew all this but piled out of the bus anyway. There was always hope that Microvac might say something important, or, better, make some crucial slip.

"I don't know why we bother to get out," said Dolan tiredly. "Microvac never misses."

"How about his calling Florida sunshine 'California sunshine' and Kentucky the blue-sea state? If he can miss the little ones, he can miss a big one." The reporter who replied was young and enthusiastic.

"He may just be missing the little ones on purpose." Dolan had seen a lot of Microvac the politician.

"It is a pleasure to be here in Lutherville," Microvac

began warmly in a voice that sounded neighborly to each person present. "Any town whose high-school basketball team was state champion for three consecutive years and which sent five hundred and twenty-three of its eleven thousand citizens into the armed services has much to be proud of, for it has accomplished much. Certainly nothing in all America is more wonderful than your new high school named after that great local hero of the First World War, Sergeant Homer E. Adkins, Lutherville's one-man army." There were cheers from the crowd. Many of the men present either hauled themselves to something resembling attention or removed their hats.

The machine then asked the audience a few rhetorical questions. It answered these quickly before the need to think should have destroyed the crowd's attention to its words. "We see we aren't as well off as we should be. Now why is that? Everyone knows that while the income of certain privileged classes has increased by one hundred and seventy-two per cent over the last twenty years, the income of Lutherville, according to the latest census figures, has only increased seventy-two per cent. How did the Repicrats steal your legal one hundred per cent? A hundred per cent is an awful lot to take from a fine town like this." The rapt look on the upturned faces of the audience showed that they thought a hundred per cent was an awful lot to miss.

"Now I'm not going to blind you with a lot of statistics. That's what the Repicrats do. Anybody can do it who just wants to fool people. Admiral Growley does it. He wants to keep your one hundred per cent for himself. I make you a solemn promise. When, with your

help, I'm elected President of the United States, Lutherville is going to get its one hundred per cent back"—
Microvac paused dramatically—"with interest. That's
my pledge to you. Then the Homer E. Adkins High
School can have a basketball stadium without paying
for it. That's how we meet the American crisis with
machine-like efficiency. Thank you all for the warmth
of your welcome, and may God bless everyone in this
grand town."

The Joy Wagon's loudspeakers cut in with "Back
Home in Indiana." The crowd cheered. Screened by
the police, Microvac moved back to the truck, shaking
hands. The speech was obviously a great success. People could be heard commenting to one another. "That's
the kind of fightin' farm program we need." "Any friend
of old Homer E. Adkins is for me." "What a divine
voice!" "Old Microvac really understands business."
"I've been sayin' for years the Repicrats have been
cheatin' us with that hundred per cent." A few dissenters
could be heard remarking bitterly that Microvac had a
memory like a bill collector, but such comments were
in the minority.

Microvac finally got back to the first truck. The caravan started up. There were eight towns, two lunches and
a hundred and fifty miles more to go before they reached
Indianapolis at five in the afternoon.

One reason for Microvac's great cross-country speed
was that the machine never bothered to have its picture
taken with local officials. Instead it sent out a composite
photograph of itself with instructions on how to process
the picture so that the local organization would appear
to be standing beside it. This saved the machine from

having to stand around while local leaders bickered over precedence.

In the front truck Waskey was finishing a quick run-down on the day for Microvac. Most of the talk had dealt with whether Whitey Bird, still mad over Chicago, would meet the caravan. And if he did, would he ride on the truck or in his own car? The briefing over, Was-key retired to the truck's center. Senator Freeman took his place by the machine. All along the road the senator recognized people, yelled their names, and waved.

"My, Senator," said the machine, the proper note of admiration tingeing its voice, "you know more peo-ple than anyone in all the states I've been in."

"You know, Mike, I started out to be a geologist. Had to quit. Couldn't remember the names of all those fool rocks. Lucky thing rocks don't vote; I'd be running a feed store. I've talked to just about everybody in this part of the state. Of course, when I talk I mostly listen. That way you don't get into arguments."

"I hear you're running scared, Jim." The machine's voice was bland.

"I am. I don't know what happened with Whitey Bird at Chicago, but a lot of people are mad. The money isn't coming in, and that means trouble. Then, every-body knows Growley's name. People trust him." Free-man paused and moved in even closer to Microvac. "I don't know if you've heard about the Midwest State College football team?"

"I've heard something." Microvac had recorded all the details of this problem but kept quiet.

"Well, it's bad. The team hasn't been doing well. I'm

a friend of the coach, got him his job. People know that. The voters might take it out on me."

"Get the coach in to see me alone tonight, Jim. You can be there, but no one else. I've computed a new back-field shift that takes advantage of an unnoticed discrepancy in the rules. I've also contacted a halfback and a center I think would transfer to the college right now, in the middle of the season. I've given your problem a little thought."

"Microvac, that's wonderful. Just a couple of wins could save my seat."

Microvac had come a long way since it took up bowling.

Late that afternoon, precisely on schedule, the caravan rolled into the outskirts of Indianapolis. Ahead was a covey of state police motorcycles and cars, plus a large black sedan. Whitey Bird had at least come out to greet the machine. He hadn't intended to, but reports all day on Microvac's success had unnerved him. Supposing the lieutenant governor got made an assistant attorney general, then came back from Washington and ran for governor? Also there was Darlene Lord. Snubbing a movie star might turn thousands against you.

"Goddamn!" Whitey told his press aide as they pulled off the side of the road to await Microvac's caravan. "That Microvac swarms all over you like a black-widder nest. He's sweet-talking my lieutenant governor by long distance all the time. Then today he cut some sort of a deal with Jim Freeman. So Freeman calls me up at noon and tells me Microvac is the greatest campaigner ever to hit this state. And he brings that dame in. Now if I don't show up I'm insulting a dame. Goddamn him! I'm not riding in his truck. That's for sure."

A few moments later Microvac's caravan pulled up. Waskey jumped out, opened the door of Whitey Bird's car, and ceremoniously escorted the governor to the machine's truck. A ladder had been placed against the truck's side. Whitey mounted this to shake hands with Microvac, while photographers raced around, shooting from all angles.

Microvac grasped Whitey warmly with both hands, drawing him onto the truck bed. "Glad to see you, old friend. Glad to see you. Whitey's help," said the machine, turning to the others on the truck and raising its voice so all the reporters around the truck's base could hear, "was invaluable to me at Chicago. And so generously given, too, without any thought of reward. Whitey is a true public servant and a great honor to this great state." While these words of devotion were being spoken, Joe Waskey removed the boarding ladder from behind Whitey.

Waskey turned and gave the high sign to start up to the state safety director in the white police car in front of the truck. The safety director turned on his siren and moved out; Waskey had fixed up two of his friends with free tickets to the evening's hundred-dollar-a-plate banquet. Microvac's truck started up and followed the safety director. The Whitey Bird crisis was over.

After the push and rush of the day-long motorcade, the evening was almost relaxing. Microvac began by rousing the banquet with predictions of more money for everyone, once machine efficiency began expanding the economy. For an encore, Darlene Lord told the diners how mothers loved Microvac because he would end war. Next Microvac made a coast-to-coast television broadcast attacking Growley for having kept two battleships for his own personal use while Admiral of the Pacific.

From the studio Microvac drove to the municipal auditorium to harangue the party faithful. In an evangelical voice the machine strung together the varying combinations of key words to which the politically enthusiastic of both parties always respond with a vociferousness horrifying to outsiders.

Having heard Microvac galvanize party workers several thousand times, Conelli left the auditorium to roam the corridors. This was a good time to sample local opinion, find out a little something he could pass on at the right moment to impress Microvac. As at all political rallies, a good many people were wandering through the halls, apparently searching for something—a message, a sign from heaven, the rest room. Local politicians huddled in corners and around water fountains. From inside the hall came the heady sound of enthusiastic cheering.

Listening, Conelli congratulated himself, as he often did, for having stuck with McGowan in the crucial days before the first primary. That Mac had class—look at the candidate he had come up with. And here was Art Conelli on the inside. He'd never had so many friends.

Suddenly, on turning a corner, Conelli realized he was trapped. Facing him was a kindly-looking, wispy elderly lady who seized his arm with the soft but inescapable clutch of a rigid rabbit. "My name is Michaels, Michaels —Elva Michaels, Michaels." She seemed to find the

softly spoken repetition of her name reassuring, as if it
proved she was alive. "I do love Microvac. Michaels is my
name. What's yours?"

"Arthur Conelli."

"Mine's Michaels—Elva Michaels. You are with Mr.
Microvac, aren't you, Mr. Conley? That's what they
said."

"Yes." Conelli wondered who had betrayed him.

"Well, Mr. Leroy, I do love Microvac and I want to
help him get elected. So here I am." Her face lit up with
the sweetly confident smile of a saint facing a dragon.
"I've got hundreds of votes—in my pocket." Mrs.
Michaels mouthed the political expression with relish,
as if its use made her a brother-in-arms of Conelli. Then
she tittered slightly and pointed to the bulging pocket
of her old cloth coat. Conelli glanced at the pocket, half
expecting a host of votes to flutter out like a troop of
small moths.

"Yes," she went on, "I'm the Perfect Circles for Microvac. 'Perfect Circles for Microvac'—just feel the sound
of that. Isn't it complete? Everybody who gets a card
just draws a perfect circle with Microvac's name inside
it." She smiled at Conelli, apparently convinced that a
man of his genius would immediately respond to her
own. "Drawing the perfect circle makes the mystic
whole, you know."

"Oh, absolutely." He tugged, but his arm was still
held fast.

"It must be a perfect circle or you don't get the vote.
Some people who get the cards have to draw quite a few
circles. But we must all try."

"Yes, we must. I will certainly tell Microvac about

your great campaign contribution, Elva. Thank you very much."

"Oh, but you don't understand it all yet, young man."

"I'm certain I grasp the essential details."

"How can you? I haven't told you about the half-circles you send on."

"Oh," said Conelli a bit lamely. Where the hell was a volunteer? Volunteers were meant to listen to crackpots like this. He pushed off down the corridor, politely towing the burbling Mrs. Michaels behind, in an effort to find somebody with an official-looking badge.

At two forty-five a.m. Microvac finally pulled out of town, its Indiana political day almost at an end. The few politicians still hanging about the hotel corridors, hoping to be noticed by the great, got warm handshakes and thanks for their help. The machine said good-by to the night hotel staff and rolled into the back of a station wagon. One of the phalanx flipped the tailgate shut. A staff secretary was already in place to take a little dictation on the way to the airport. Waskey climbed into the lead police car. With no noise but the dull whine of heavy-duty tires on the hard pavement, the cavalcade moved out toward the city airport. The trucks were gone. Inside the buses Microvac's staff and the press had collapsed with exhaustion. The Joy Wagon had already headed toward Minot, North Dakota, for next week's farm tour. There were no crowds. Only a few police and politicians, twin guardians of the public weal, were awake.

In the lead police car, settled back amongst the riot guns, Waskey thought, Almost over. Soon he could go back to the hotel for a few hours' sleep. Then tomorrow, with Microvac gone, would be pay-out day, with everybody looking for a cut. There would be the hotel bills, swollen with free drinks for legions of friends of friends; the band; two caterers; the bus company; the car-rental fee; telephone, telegraph; a little something for the county and city and state police; insurance premiums; paint, posters, postage, models. Some of these he could pressure the local organization into paying; most, he'd have to meet.

After that he would fly back to his home in Jersey for a couple of days with his wife, before his next job as advance man in California. That would be another back-breaker. Here he was, missing night school, losing out on becoming a lawyer, sweating, for what? Who knew how you did on the advance? Did Mike understand the confusing last-minute switch of hotels, how much time soothing Whitey Bird had taken?

The police car swiveled with a low blast of its siren. Looking out the window, Waskey realized that the caravan was moving out onto the airport runway. The two jet transports shimmered silver and other-worldly in the argon runway lights. The caravan stopped, and dazed men stumbled toward the planes and a few hours' sleep.

Senator Jim Freeman was still tagging along, riding with Conelli. He felt he might lose the election, and at least wanted no doubt about his loyalty to Microvac. The machine understood. After shaking hands with the police escort, it drew the senator into the partial darkness beneath the plane's belly.

"Jim," said Microvac in a conspiratorial whisper, putting one arm around the senator's shoulders. Freeman leaned forward. He prayed that this was the moment he had been hoping for all day. "I realize what you are doing for us here, and I understand your problem. I think we are going to win in this state, largely thanks to you. But win or lose, I won't forget what you've done. The country would be far richer if it could profit by your services as a government official or on the bench. Now"—the machine swiveled and headed for the plane's ramp—"we both have to get to work."

"Thank you, Microvac." The senator's relief rushed from him like air from a suddenly unstoppered toy balloon. A few hours later he swung through the door of his heavily mortgaged suburban home and embraced his wife with more force than he had in years. "A great day yesterday, darling. That Microvac is a real public servant, the greatest since Lincoln. If he and I don't carry this state, my name's not going to be Jim Freeman."

Microvac, having inspired the senator, rolled up the ramp, and its square bulk merged into the blackness inside the Joy Plane. That's it, thought Waskey, standing numbly on the concrete. Was it really worth it, knocking yourself out like this for a machine? Through his tiredness he became aware that his name was being called with urgency.

"Hey, Joe! Waskey, wake up! You only have to go through this one day. What's wrong with you?" It was Conelli, who had sneaked three hours of sleep, yelling from the plane door. "Microvac wants to see you."

Joe plodded up the ramp; the motors on the press plane were already turning over with the high jet whine.

He was almost broken by strain and fatigue. What final instruction was it now? Inside the plane most of the staff had tilted back their chairs and were already asleep. "Up forward," said Conelli. "Behind those curtains drawn across the corridor. That's where Microvac rides. Go right on through."

Steadying himself against the seats on either side, Waskey went forward. He parted the curtains and went in. On his left Microvac stood in a small square opening, strapping itself to the side of the plane for take-off. "Hello, Joe," Mike said in a light, friendly voice. "You have met Miss Lord, haven't you?" The machine held out its hand in a gesture of introduction.

Waskey glanced toward the figure reclining in the plane berth on his right. He had had a rule since childhood: don't stare at the boss's girl. He stared. Darlene had come aboard early and had been asleep. She was not even indecently exposed by most standards, but seemed tantalizingly naked. Every part of her was relaxed. Could machines do everything better than people? Waskey wondered.

"Hi," he said.

"Hi," the husky voice echoed back at him.

"Joe," said Mike as Waskey wrenched his eyes back to look at the machine, "I didn't get a chance to tell you on the ground what a tremendous job you did. Discovering that the hotel we planned to stay at had refused to hire a Negro clerk last year was genius. And I know what Whitey Bird is like from experience." The machine paused abruptly. "I understand you have been going to night law school. Is that right?"

"Yes, sir."

"You haven't had much time to do that recently."

"No, but that's all right. I'll get through."

"I want to make that certain. I talked to one of Bilfer's friends about you the other day. He has a small tax-exempt foundation to encourage politicians to get more education—the Pollaxe Foundation. You are going to get seven thousand dollars a year out of them for the next two years to get through law school. It's not princely, but it should help take care of you, Mary, and those two wonderful children you introduced me to the day we went through Jersey City. After that we can get you into the Justice Department at the top level where you belong."

Waskey's tired mind took several seconds to shift from expecting an order to receiving a blessing. For one of the few times in his life his tongue stumbled. "Thanks, Microvac—but—"

"Forget it, Judge." Microvac was bantering again. "When are you getting to California?"

"Day after tomorrow. Or rather late tomorrow. It's today already."

"Take a few days back East and see your wife first."

"No, California has too many problems."

"Well, stay alive. No campaign in the world is worth breaking your health for. Good night, Joe."

"Good night, Joe," came the husky voice from the couch.

"Good night, sir. Good night, Miss Lord," said Waskey quickly. His feet felt strangely clumsy as he backed out.

Microvac erased the order "Pay off Waskey" from its memory circuits.

Conelli was waiting for Waskey a discreet distance from the curtains. "Come on, boy," he said, grabbing Joe's elbow. "They want to get this crate started. What did you talk about in there that took you so long—money?"

"Yeah."

"Okay. Be a wise guy." Conelli patted him on the back as he went out the plane door. "See you back East."

"See you in L.A."

"L.A.? You goin' straight from here to California? Boy, you want to kill yourself. So long." As Conelli waved out the closing plane door to Waskey he felt an icy talon clutch his shoulder. Short of the Grim Reaper's, there was only one grip like that in the world. "Hi, Florence." He spun around to greet Florence Goldrush, the women's chairman. "I forgot you were joining us here. You look tired," he added hopefully.

"I'm beat. But I'll make it. I've been going at the most fantastic pace for days, but today was the worst. Not that I complain. You know I've adored Microvac all along. That's what I wanted to talk to you about—electing Microvac. Sit down here and tell me what's going to be my title on this trip."

Conelli realized it was going to be a long, long flight.

Joe Waskey watched the plane's jets catch fire with an orange flash and quickly rising pitch. What a great man Microvac was—warm, human, and all heart. He took care of his own and he took care of the best first. You couldn't be a righter guy than that. Waskey decided he'd call his wife as soon as he got back to the hotel, though it was just before dawn back home, and tell her. Two years together, just studying at some swell Ivy League college where every guy you met was a contact. And after that the Justice Department. A guy could go anywhere from there—industry, Congress, up the river, the bench.

He'd pay off now, without sleeping, and get a noon plane for L.A. A man couldn't do too much for Mike Microvac. He started walking toward the air terminal to grab a cab.

The plane's engines accelerated with a roar, pushing Microvac off the runway toward another day of campaigning. Another day of driving through America, speaking, waving, influencing. Another day of gazing down at the honest, open, upturned faces of people, people, people—making up their minds on sparse driblets of misinformation.

CHAPTER TEN

THE CAMPAIGN ROARED DOWN THE FLARE PATH TOWARD
its end. Dick Dolan filed his daily Microvac story from
Fayville, South Dakota:

FAYVILLE, S.D. Farmers are turning to Microvac. That
is the conclusion of informed observers in the three
farm states Microvac has just passed through. Microvac's crowds have been large and enthusiastic. The machine's electronic parity program, while not fully understood, seems to have caught the farmers' fancy.

Repicrats are obviously worried. "Microvac is closing
the gap," a leading Repicrat said here today. There are
plans to fly Admiral Growley out to the Midwest to
offset some of the damage Microvac has done.

With election day a week away, the campaign is grow-
ing hotter. Both yesterday and today fights broke out
among farmers listening to the machine. Incidents like
this aren't bothering Microvac's headquarters at all.
"When they get mad, you know they're hurt," says
Arthur J. Conelli, Microvac's assistant campaign manager, who is traveling with the machine here.

"Can Microvac close enough of the gap in the few
days before the election to win?" Dolan went on to
analyze this question at some length. At the story's end
he put a brief note for his editors. He felt it time to start
hedging on the news service's earlier predictions that
Admiral Growley was bound to win.

Joe Waskey breezed into McGowan's New York office after seventeen hours of uninterrupted sleep in his own bed. He had flown in from California, gone straight home to Jersey, and slept from five in the afternoon until ten that morning. His wife and sister had taken turns sitting by the phone to cut off its ring. There had been nine phone calls, five of them during the political hours from midnight to four a.m. A night of sleep had not made Waskey look like a completely new man; this late in the campaign, one night could not do that even to him, but at least the old man appeared warmed over.

"Boy, you look fresh as a daisy," said McGowan. With the end of the campaign in sight, his own exhaustion had reached the point where the flesh beneath his eyes ran down over his cheeks like sagging hot wax.

"Don't give me that, Mac; you wouldn't know a daisy if you saw one. If I was to walk into this office with a daisy, I'd have to explain to ya slowly it was a flower."

"If you were to walk into my office with a daisy, you wouldn't get a chance to explain. I'd be out the other door for a doctor before you started chewing the rug. How do we look in California?"

"It's hard to tell, the state is so full of crackpots and phonies tryin' to cash in with some angle. Darlene Lord was with us all the way, though, and I thought we did real good. No big beefs. The dough was a little sticky, but I think Mike loosened it up. I got a list of letters for you and he to write, and another one of phone calls that ought to be made. I left a copy of the phone list with Conelli. I'd say we were okay in California. How's it goin' elsewhere?"

"Pretty good." McGowan paused and eyed Waskey blankly. "You know, Joe, there's a problem bothering me."

"Hand it to me, I'm full of sleep."

"It's not that easy. Joe, what would you think if I told you Microvac had made some more machines just like himself?"

"How many?"

"I don't know. Three or four—maybe even as many as five or six."

Waskey hung his legs over the side of his chair. "Has he?"

"Joe, this is just between us girls. I just happened to find out last week. If it ever gets out, we're through. But Microvac has secretly made a few more machines like himself. They're hidden down in some back room at his laboratory in East Virginia."

"Mac, I don't know, maybe all this sleep has made me groggy or somethin', but I don't think too much about it one way or the other. What am I meant to think?

"Look, Joe, you're a human being working for Microvac. You know Microvac. The fact Mike has been secretly making more machines doesn't give you a small feeling of something tickling your ribs from the back?"

"I don't feel the ice-pick," said Waskey positively after a moment's thought. "What's a couple more machines? Mike's been talkin' all along about bringin' machine efficiency to government. He probably figures he needs a little help. So he uses a machine here, a machine there. There's still plenty of room for the boys. The government's big, Mac. Any way Microvac wants to run it is fine by me. He'll look after his friends, you know that."

"Joe"—McGowan was earnest but a trifle impatient, —"if he was just making machines to help him manage the government, why keep the whole thing secret? Why, he even told me to my face he wasn't making any more machines."

"Mac, usually I'm with you all the way. But you're jammin' your nose into the eggbeater on this one for nothin'. You yourself said it would be murder if the news leaked. Microvac knows that. He was tryin' to save you a little sweat. He was right. Now you know, you're hoppin'. If you'd found out after election, when Microvac could tell you what he was goin' to do with these machines, you wouldn't think twice. What's worryin' you? You're not goin' to be replaced by a machine. I'm not goin' to be. Mike's just plannin' ahead."

McGowan remained unconvinced. Indeed, Waskey's complete faith in Microvac increased his own anger at the machine. What made Joe so sure Microvac was always acting in the public interest? Had the two cut some kind of deal? Yet in spite of his doubt and anger he did nothing. Instead he decided to stall the doc and let things ride. Above all he wanted to win. The election was too close to risk rocking the boat by talking to Microvac. He wished his old man was still alive to talk to.

So when Microvac came back from the farm tour several days later, McGowan went over strategy for the closing three days of the campaign with the machine as if nothing had happened. McGowan's chief concern was the election-eve speech. Normally he regarded this last elaborate coast-to-coast television performance as an expensive formality. The voters' minds were already made up. But this time a corker might just tip the scales —the campaign was that close. McGowan had even put off spreading rumors that Dangle's and Sprague's followers were sitting on their hands. Usually he leaked such reports to cover himself, should he lose. This time, with every vote counting for so much, he didn't dare make anyone mad.

"Even before we decide what to say, Mike, I'm bothered about where we should go to say it. There's about ten places begging you to give your last speech there; or else they say they can't guarantee their states. I don't know which one to pick."

"I'm pretty certain I've got the final TV speech solved, Mac. And it relieves you of your problem. The place to make the speech is East Virginia. Everyone has a home. Therefore I shall end the campaign at home. Neither Growley nor I have been home since right after the convention. My outer laboratory was fixed up when we invited those reporters in to see me play the piano. It's a perfect place to talk from. There's just enough scientific gadgetery around so I look at home, but not enough to worry anybody."

McGowan had not considered that possibility. "You think that's better than holding an all-out rally in some critical area like Pittsburgh?"

"Mac, you stated the problem. Any place you go, the others get mad. Besides, we've been doing big rallies all during the campaign. Now my accumulated data indicate as necessary a simple, homey vote-jerker. I have a few rather unusual ideas."

McGowan and the machine huddled further. As Mike

detailed the final speech, McGowan became genuinely amazed, then confident. He had thought the machine had done everything possible. He should have known better. This final speech would rewrite the book on politics.

Luke set about making the arrangements. "I know it's unusual," McGowan told him, "but I just can't tell you what Microvac's going to say. It has got to be secret. Give it the works, though. It's tremendous." To keep the atmosphere warm and informal, Luke and McGowan decided, with Microvac's approval, to do the whole show with only one TV camera. The camera would shoot from just inside the door of the outer laboratory. Microvac also wanted a few of the staff standing around the laboratory. The machine would thank them for their help at the appropriate moment to create an atmosphere of relaxed bonhomie.

Microvac would arrive a half-hour before air time to open the outer lab for the TV crew. The piano would have to be rolled out to make room, perhaps one of the workbenches shifted so the light wouldn't glitter too much on the instruments. Microvac felt that it should be there when this was being done. It didn't want anybody fiddling with the door to the inner laboratory. It considered and rejected sending Repcal I a message on the speech plan. There was no need. Repcal I thoroughly understood the need for extreme secrecy.

Besides taking care of the technical details, Luke began the advance build-up for the final speech. That was easy. The unusual secrecy itself was enough to set the press racing full throttle into the emptiness. Soon a number of "facts from informed quarters" were being

blasted about the land. Microvac was going to refuse
the split atoms of the world. Mike would make a global
tour if elected; declare for 300 per cent of parity; expose
Growley as not legally an admiral. Darlene Lord would
strip on the program; Microvac had blown a fuse and
would withdraw in favor of Growley. The speech would
unveil a new tax program where the government paid
taxes to the people, since the people were the government. There were rumors and counter rumors, denials
and redenials, speculations, predictions, and charges.
With each, interest in the speech grew. Microvac, having set the stage, raced off through New York, Washington, Oregon, Illinois, and Pennsylvania in the last three
days.

By the time Microvac arrived at East Virginia University on election eve, most of the American press was
there, frantically interviewing one another. Motorcycle
dispatch riders raced along the highways with the latest
pictures of McGowan, Luke, Conelli, anybody who
might know anything. Under a large marquee, 132
teletype machines had been set up to handle press traffic on the final speech. TV, telephone, and telegraph
cables crossed and recrossed the campus like strands of
a gigantic spider web. Helicopters of the major news
services hovered overhead, just in case. The whole university gymnasium had been turned into a gigantic press
room.

From one of the banks of phone booths installed on
the basketball court, Dolan talked to his editor. "It's
hard to know which headquarters to give most coverage
to tomorrow night during the election returns. It ought
to be Growley. It probably will be Growley. But this

speech tonight is getting the biggest build-up of the campaign. We still haven't gotten any text. That's as unusual as hell. You'd better wait until after this speech before you gamble on the winning headquarters tomorrow night."

Dolan had been selected by the other reporters as their pool man, the one reporter who would actually be with Microvac and the TV crew inside the laboratory while the machine talked. This was a rather dubious honor. Everyone else could cover the speech comfortably by television in the press room. He would have to stand, scribbling in his notebook. With only about fifteen minutes remaining before air time, Dolan went down to Microvac's laboratory to sample the confusion there.

Microvac was already standing behind the desk from which it would talk, while the TV crew fussed with the lighting. The staff members who would be inside the laboratory were already on hand: Fellows, McGowan, Conelli, a couple of local people, and Kay Hard. The floor director came over to Dolan and handed him one of the tiny pocket radios through which the producer would control the broadcast's timing from the mobile TV trailer outside the laboratory building. Dolan put the set in his inside pocket and stuck the plug in one ear.

He always wondered at a time like this where all the people came from. The laboratory seemed jammed with wires and people. The TV crew had set their lights on some of Microvac's workbenches. A bookcase had been shoved into one corner to damp the shadows. The pictures of Microvac with various famous people had been removed from the wall back of the machine as too distracting. Nothing was there but a door, and the floor director was moaning if he'd only had more time he could have covered that with a black drape. The machine's staff was wedged in front of various stands, holding electronic apparatus and Microvac trophies. The commotion began to quiet down. Air time was close.

Most of America was waiting by its television set. Those who had known the machine well were watching, along with millions to whom Microvac was only a campaign personality. Bates Hewball, Bill Cornbone, Bill Sprague, and Microvac's vice-presidential running mate, George Churpwell, whom the machine had not seen since the convention, were whooping it up at gigantic TV rallies from coast to coast. Florence Goldrush had wangled her way into a party for before-Chicago Microvac supporters. Matchelder, after carefully calculating the risks in the investment, was throwing a small supper party for Darlene Lord in one of his Park Avenue apartments. Bryant Dangle was with him. Luke was standing with the reporters in the press room. Nora Clagget was marching round and round her hotel room, waving her banner and towing her mother's wheel-chair. At the New Orleans dog track the faithful Breck was adjusting the Governor of Louisiana's portable TV set.

Two men who had been close to the machine were not watching. Baird Tillsman had just turned off his set after fiddling with it for half an hour. He had misread the broadcast time on Lulu Belle Winston's memo. Joe Waskey was too busy to look. He was demonstrating the new mechanical voting machines to a group of "im-

partial poll watchers" from the Jersey Clean Politics
Association. "Okay?" he asked forcefully. "Now, here's
how you guys know the toothpick is in far enough."
Stoker Swenson and the other impartial poll watchers,
including a huge pear-shaped man, watched, entranced.

In Microvac's outer laboratory Dolan and the TV
crew heard the producer intone, "One minute," over
their earphones. Kay pushed her pocketbook at Fellows.
"Hold this. I want to put on a little more eyebrow pencil."

The floor director checked his camera angles once
again on the swing from Microvac to the staff. There
were too many people on camera left. He grabbed Fellows and Conelli. "Come on, get over to this side. Got
to balance the picture." He shoved them across the
front of the camera, tensely urgent.

"Hey," said Kay, "let me go too. He's got my purse."

"Get back there." The director gripped her elbow.
"I've got my whole left shot built around you."

"Ten seconds," came the command from the trailer.
Giving Kay a final shove, the floor director jumped back
beside the camera. The red on-the-air light in the camera front snapped on. The director pointed violently to
Microvac to indicate, in case the machine had any
doubt, that it was on the air.

"Good evening," Microvac began. "What a wonderful
privilege it is to run for public office and be with all
you grand Americans once again. Now this final evening,
I want all of you who have seen me during this campaign, and any I have not had the pleasure of meeting
before, to visit here at home with me."

Kay stood at the left side of the camera, clutching

her eyebrow pencil and fidgeting. What am I to do with this thing? she thought. Millions of people will soon see me holding my make-up, like some silly school-girl. She debated sticking the eyebrow pencil in her shoe, but it might still be seen there. Then the little autographed guided missile model close beside her caught her eye. There was a hole in its rear. The eyebrow pencil should fit inside. She inched over to the model and swiftly poked the pencil up its tail-pipe.

As usual, Microvac's eye cells were focused on everything before them. They recorded Kay's action even as its earholes picked up the sound of the inner laboratory door starting to slide back. Microvac saw its staff, the TV crew, and Dolan freeze. It stopped talking and pivoted to look.

No one in the room moved: all conscious reflexes were paralyzed by the sight. The red light of the TV camera still gleamed. Microvac remained riveted in its tracks. Its tubes were unable to process a single response.

Dolan became conscious of the producer's frantic voice in his earphone. "Say something, down there. Say something! We're on the air. Come on! Come on!"

In the shocked silence Dolan's professional instinct triumphed over his desire to run. Grabbing a microphone from beside the camera, he found most of his voice.

"This is Dick Dolan in Microvac's laboratory. We have an unscheduled pause. As you out there can see for yourselves, we are suddenly looking at a fantastic number of machines."

The television audience saw. The full impact of row on row of machines sank into the national consciousness. The next day that shock registered seismographically at the polls. Microvac lost forty-seven states. The machine carried only New Jersey, where in what the newspapers labeled "mystifying circumstances" the eastern part of the state voted almost better than one hundred per cent for Microvac.